A NEW YORK

Cassie kocca

About *A New York Love Story*

Giving a present is not always easy. Clover O'Brian knows that only too well: her job consists of helping people in the arduous task of choosing unusual gifts. Christmas is coming, New York is buzzing, and Clover, who has always loved the festive period, savours the atmosphere.

Cade Harrison already has everything in life. A Hollywood actor, he is handsome, rich, famous and popular. Success, however, has its downsides; having just emerged from a disastrous relationship with an actress, he feels a need to hide away in an area unfrequented by stars, in an apartment lent him by a friend, far from prying eyes – especially those of tabloid reporters. But as chance will have it, the apartment in question is right opposite the one occupied by Clover, who until now has seen Hollywood actors only on the big screen. Two quite different lives meet by chance, at the most exhilarating time of year…

To those who still believe, in spite of everything.

1

The sound of children's laughter echoed through the streets. Everywhere you could hear the general gaiety of young and old alike, typical of a festive holiday gathering.

In a small residential neighborhood of Staten Island, families celebrated Thanksgiving. They chatted amiably around tables loaded with delicious offerings: stuffed turkeys, pumpkin pies and sweet potatoes. Outside, children enjoyed a cold sunny day at the end of November, running and trying to catch one another; but the Stevenson children were laughing louder than the others. A strange *human turkey* was running after them.

"So! You want to eat me? I'll show you, cannibals! I'm sick of seeing my poor siblings cooked on your tables!"

With a croaky voice, imitating turkey gobble-gobble sounds, Clover O'Brian, delighted by their terrified shouts, was running after the three seven year old rascals on the lawn in front of the church.

"Which of you has eaten the most turkey today?" She emphasized this with a loud "Ooolullu! Ooolulluuu!"

"I did! I did!" Sam, the one missing two front teeth, shouted. "I had two servings!"

"Ahh! It's not hard to believe it with those missing teeth! So, I will eat you first! Ooolulluuu!" She rushed at him with her head down, making the child scream with excitement. Then she continued running after the other two little ones... She began to feel out of breath, but she liked hearing the children laugh and – by the way – she didn't have anything better to do. She was always on her own on Thanksgiving Day. Actually, to be honest, she was alone for every holiday.

She couldn't really say she had a *family*, and of course her few friends spent the holidays with their loved ones. Often they invited her, but she preferred to pass on these invitations and find alternative ways of spending those days. Crashing family parties only reminded her of what she missed out on and she didn't like gloomy thoughts.

Happiness was almost a duty for Clover, especially at this time of year. She adored Christmas. She loved the atmosphere in December. It was the best month of the year for her, and she made great efforts not to let anyone spoil those sacred thirty days, even if it meant celebrating them by herself.

Since her father's death ten years ago, Clover had slowly grown accustomed to solitude. It wasn't that the O'Brians expressed any great cheerfulness during the holidays when she was growing up: her family didn't seem to have either a strong inclination towards joy, or much of a Christmas spirit. But still, she never lost the childish excitement that made her smile like an idiot in front of dozens of colorful packages under a lighted Christmas tree. And she protected this feeling with all her strength from the cynicism and disenchantment of others.

Her mother had always hated Christmas. She detested having to organize an impressive party for guests, find gifts for everybody, and smile incessantly at relatives and friends. All this created a lot of tension from which her father wisely distanced himself. Since she had become a widow things had got even worse. Nadia O'Brian had stopped organizing any kind of party or event, but she did accept other people's invitations.

Since his marriage, her brother Patrick had lost any interest in Christmas, considering it just a children's holiday. Honestly, many other things had changed too, and none for the better. He had withdrawn into himself, focusing only on his work and his children. He'd forgotten the strong bond they used to have. Clover thought about Patrick with nostalgia and sadness. She was left with just memories. Because her sister-in-law didn't especially like her, her relationship with her brother had weakened and they saw each other only sporadically.

However – despite some sense of loneliness and her childhood memories – she didn't regret the estrangement from her family. It had allowed Clover to put the right distance between her need for serenity and lightness and their tendency towards pessimism and melodrama. The death of her paternal grandmother had given her the opportunity to leave home and move away, for she had inherited the little bungalow where she had lived for three years now. Leaving Maine had been a blessing, reducing the encounters with her family to almost zero.

Now the Christmas holidays had become the domain of Patrick and his wife Sienna. Every year the O'Brian family got together at their country house. For a few days they all pretended to get along and enjoy the festivities for the children's sake. Since she wasn't very good at pretending and hiding inconvenient truths, she wasn't welcome at these family reunions. But she didn't care much. She remembered the torment of earlier years, when she used to go to those gatherings. There were always arguments and long faces that eventually ended with headaches and sadness. Since then, there was an unspoken agreement between herself and Patrick: he invited her to Christmas Eve dinner and Christmas Day lunch, and she pretended to have other commitments; so it all became just a matter of sending gifts to everybody. This was the only thing that kept her from being permanently crossed out of the family tree: she was damned good at finding gifts!

"Clover, you're too slow! You can't catch us!"

Mark, the smarter of the Stevensons, woke her up from her reverie, bringing her back to reality with a jolt.

"I think I had too many children for lunch! I need to get some rest. I will eat you another time…"

"Attack!" They all shouted together, running towards her.

Laughing, she turned to run away and found an unexpected obstacle. All of a sudden an object materialized in front of her, obscuring her view. She bounced off it and fell over on the grass.

"Damn!"

"Are you ok?" At the sound of this voice, Clover looked up, a hand was extending to help her rise. The hand was the elegant extension of an arm which was attached to a well-proportioned body, covered – but not completely – with an elegant jacket.

"Bloody hell!" She got up without taking the hand, "are you Wolverine?"

"No, that's Hugh Jackman."

"Well, by the feel of your chest, I would say you're made of *adamantium* too!"

"Was the impact so hard? Should I call an ambulance?" He sounded amused.

Clover finally looked up at his face and she almost fell down again.

Even with the woolly hat and the collar of his jacket turned up, it was impossible not to recognize him. Cade Harrison, the famous Hollywood actor, was in front of her in all his handsome glory, with a slightly surprised and amused expression… waiting for something…? Maybe he was expecting an enthusiastic reaction, his was enough to stop her from dropping her jaw in amazement like a silly woman.

She stood up, all five foot, four inches of her – thank god the boots made her look a little taller – and brushed off her coat.

"I didn't expect to stumble into a wall on my way home. I wasn't prepared. One shouldn't materialize all of a sudden behind people, especially when one is your size!"

"I won't forget that advice next time I decide to go out for a walk…"

Clover raised her eyebrows, "Do *you* live *here*?"

"I hope there isn't a law yet that forbids people with an imposing physique to live in peaceful neighborhoods…"

"I've never *seen* you before." When she saw Harrison's expression, she waved her hand and added, "I mean, around here, and I've been living in this neighborhood for a while now… I would for sure have noticed a famous face!"

"A friend kindly lent me his house for the holidays," he smiled, flashing his very white teeth – perfect enough to deserve a place of honor on the wall of a dentist's office.

Clover suddenly wondered if Cade Harrison had ever been in an ad for toothpaste, but no… he had been in an ad for a perfume. Now she remembered: six feet of sculpted muscles and tanned skin, lying down on pure white silk sheets with a slender, tall, very beautiful, sexy model… On the contrary she must have looked like a wreck: bundled up in a shapeless coat, with a long pink scarf that clashed with her red hair, her bottom stained with grass and dirty hands. She hoped that at least there was no food stuck in her teeth!

"What is a stellar actor like you doing here? I thought the very rich and famous always went to Aspen!" Clover regretted this as soon as she said it… Why the hell should she make herself ridiculous in front of a man like him?

Harrison seemed to be taken by surprise. He was certainly used to a completely different kind of approach from people he met on the street: requests for autographs, selfies, and hysterical cries. He didn't expect to be harassed by a crazy woman who ran around making turkey calls, and addressed him as an unwelcome guest in the neighborhood.

"That is exactly what everybody expects," he answered, putting his hands in his pockets. "And for that reason I am not going to Aspen or to whatever other place it is where celebrities go."

"Okay, I get it… and so where is your friend's house here? Maybe I know it."

"It's over there…"

Clover's eyes followed the direction Cade Harrison was pointing in.

"But it's in front of my house!"

Cade moved his gaze towards the small bungalow, and Clover almost wanted to jump in front of him to prevent him from looking. Compared to her neighbor's three-story house, hers really looked like a dump, and she could only imagine how it looked to this super wealthy, famous actor. She was slowly doing some work, but she couldn't afford a real renovation. Actually, she had only started to do inside improvements: now the rooms looked fresher and more cheerful and modern. But on the outside the small Victorian house still had the melancholic air of decay it had when her grandmother lived there.

She tried to convince herself she didn't care about a stranger's opinion and continued the conversation. "I'm only acquainted with your friend… anyway, it will be interesting to have you in the neighborhood. It's very rare to meet VIP's or celebrities around here."

"Honestly, I would prefer it if the word didn't spread…" He looked around with a circumspect and worried expression, "I'm here for some peace."

Clover tried to restrain herself from laughing. "Do you think you can keep your presence secret in a place like this? You should have thought about that *before* showing your face on half the world's screens! All the neighborhood will know in a few hours that Cade Harrison is among us regular human beings!"

Suddenly he stiffened up and looked tense. "If you are thinking of selling me out to journalists for money, I can tell you that they don't pay as much as you imagine."

"Wait… what kind of person do you think I am?!" Clover burst out. "I'm definitely poor compared to you, but I don't need to bother others to make some extra money!" Annoyed, she stepped back. "Have a good stay, Mr Harrison."

When she turned she saw the little Stevensons watching them. Clover went over to them with a tense smile. "What are you doing still here?"

"Who were you talking to?" Andy asked, curiously.

"I saw him on TV!" Mark exclaimed.

Clover glanced at Cade. He was still there, staring at them with his blue eyes and shaking his head...

"No Mark. He's not who you think he is. I thought the same thing too at first, and asked him. He got really upset. He doesn't like it that everybody confuses him with that third-rate actor! Yes, he looks like him, but if you look at him carefully, you'll see that he's not the same guy. He's not as tall, he's much less tanned and not nearly as handsome as the actor on TV; not even as simpatico!" She spoke with a tone of conspiracy, but her voice was loud enough to be heard by *Mr Star*.

"Then I don't care about him!" The child said, focusing his attention on her again. "Do you want to play?"

"No, I need to go home. But watch out: sooner or later I will eat you... all of you!" She scared them off by baring her teeth, and shouting, they ran away.

Clover turned towards Cade Harrison, "Don't worry, I diverted their curiosity."

"On the contrary, I think you increased it. In a few minutes – in those children's home – everybody will be talking about the man *who looks like a famous actor*, and they will all want to check him out."

"Then, next time you're looking for peace and privacy go to a desert or wear a mask! You can't force people not to notice you..." Clover sighed. "However, if it helps, this neighborhood is inhabited mostly by kids and middle aged people. It's unlikely that you'll find a hysterical woman at your door asking you to autograph her butt!"

She noticed he was deeply embarrassed by her reference to the episode that all the tabloids had gleefully reported, and her animosity somehow weakened.

"I've always wondered how you can keep an autograph on your skin intact. I guess you must avoid washing that part of the body: a kind of disturbing idea, don't you think?"

"In *that specific case*, the autograph was immediately

6

transformed into a tattoo." He was trying to restrain an ironic smile, while turnng towards home.

"Oh god! Are people really willing to go that far?" Clover laughed with incredulity. She was following him and was satisfied to have found something to embarrass the *Prince of Hollywood* with. This was the nickname that the gossip magazines had given him. "Now I understand your desire to stay away from people. It can't be easy to have to sign a bottom every time you go out for groceries!"

"It's not something that happens to me every day," Cade replied and kept walking. "And anyway, these are displays of affection from my fans. I can't complain: I owe my success to them."

Clover had doubts about the sincerity of this. It seemed as if he were acting in a screenplay, as though he'd been instructed to answer these kinds of questions in a diplomatic way.

"If this is how you feel, then you would enjoy meeting a client of mine, she's really sweet. She has the biggest butt you can imagine! I think she would probably like to have her right butt cheek autographed by you, if you would sacrifice yourself in the name of love for a great fan of yours…"

"Very funny."

"It could become a new trend, actually a full time job for you: the *buttocks autograph artist*. I'm sure it would be a big success in Hollywood."

When they reached the gate of his villa, Cade Harrison looked at her, said: "If you have finished with your bullshit, I will say goodbye…"

"Oh! Already? Don't you want to sign my butt too? Maybe you would like to make a dedication on my back… if I remember correctly, I read somewhere that you did that too."

"If you have an ice pick, I can start right now."

"Such cruelty! I thought you just said that your fans' requests are displays of affection, therefore they are sacred…"

"I'm not responsible for people's craziness. I just do to my best to please them, within limits and quickly." He sighed. "However, you shouldn't believe everything you read in magazines: seventy per cent of those articles are pure fantasy."

Clover faked surprise. "Are you telling me that it's *not* true that you keep a spaceship in the garage of your mansion in LA?"

"No, I'm sorry to disappoint you…"

"And don't even have a girlfriend in every continent?"

"I would be crazy! I would have to support each and every one of them."

"… and you are not even an alien sent to earth to inseminate American women to improve our race?"

Now he looked puzzled. "Where did you read *that*?"

She laughed, "On a website!"

"We are bordering on the ridiculous."

"Such a disappointment! You showed up here to deprive me of all my beliefs…"

"You already know that Santa Claus doesn't exist, right?"

Clover, melodramatically, put her hand on her heart, "That is a low blow! You are a monster."

"And you're a nutcase!" He opened the gate with a sarcastic smile. "My friend should have warned me of the danger of having you as a neighbor, when he offered me his house."

Suddenly Clover got tense. "Your friend doesn't know me at all…"

"Or perhaps it's exactly for this reason that he spends so much time out of town!"

"Maybe…" Her good mood had disappeared in a flash. "I've got to go now. Have happy holidays, Mr Harrison."

She left, heading to her house. She tried to appear dignified, walking with confidence and purpose, not daring to look back. She had acted like a fool in front of *Mr Hollywood* and didn't want to give him even more of an advantage. She cursed through her teeth at the gate, when it squeaked in a sinister way, but she walked on with her head held high. Only when she was in the sanctuary of her house did she allow herself to turn. She looked through the peep hole on the front door. She couldn't help feeling attracted by the magnetic presence of that actor on the other side of the street.

"Bravo Clover! Great performance…" she mumbled to herself, watching as he climbed the steps with a feline grace. "You find yourself face to face with a famous movie star, and you become aggressive and start talking about butts and magazine rumors, mercilessly provoking him!"

As soon as she saw him disappear into his house, she moved away from the door, taking off her scarf, her hands trembling. Maybe her mother wasn't so wrong to be ashamed of her.

Nadia O'Brian was intent on living life and looking her best as she faced her middle years. She had decided to become *someone*. Actually she was only the testimonial for an anti-aging brand of cosmetic products, but to be in this milieu often gave her a chance to meet celebrities. Regardless of what they might think of her, she liked to count them among her dearest friends. Of course Clover never met any of these VIP's: after all, her mother had a *reputation* to maintain. Clover, with her unrestrained attitude and rude behavior, was too much of a liability. She always exhorted her daughter to try to be more elegant and sophisticated, but without any success. Clover didn't really care about appearances. She didn't spend hours in front of the mirror, trying to match makeup, clothes and accessories. Although her style couldn't really be called classy, nobody could accuse her of lacking honesty, or of playing the game. Ok, maybe she was too impulsive, sometimes even reckless, but what was the point of trying to be the new Grace Kelly? Whom should she enchant? Her mother? Truthfully, she had tried to, but without obtaining any more attention or consideration, she had given up. She seldom regretted being who she was, but now at this moment she thought that maybe a bit more elegance and grace would have made a better impression on Cade Harrison... "Who cares?" She thought aloud, collapsing on her sofa. She would survive without too much difficulty, even though a perfect famous stranger – who she probably wouldn't meet again – would judge her. She sighed and turned the TV on. She had no intention of letting anybody spoil her day. She had a funny movie to watch, delicious sweets to eat, and a whole lazy afternoon to enjoy.

Someone else might have considered her to be pathetically sad: all alone on holiday, sitting on a gnarled old couch, with a movie and a bowl of junk food, but Clover consoled herself thinking that even the Prince of Hollywood was all alone too, in a not especially glamourous building, in an unpretentious neighborhood. And for sure he wouldn't be considered pathetic: people would say he was celebrating Thanksgiving in an *intimate* and *discreet* way. Perfect! She was also celebrating in an intimate and discreet way. She didn't need anyone else in order to be happy.

2

His telephone didn't stop ringing. This was something that really bothered him. He had only been in New York for four days, yet it seemed that everybody needed to contact him urgently!

His agent had called him at least thirty times, to remind him of things that needed his immediate attention: contract drafts, screenplays to read, charity commitments and TV appearances. His press office kept calling to ask for statements for the journalists, following the scandal that had forced him to disappear from sight for a little while – as if he hadn't made enough declarations to the press already in the last month! His worried parents continued to call, asking how he was doing. And now, on top everything else... *her*.

Cade looked at the screen of his cell phone and saw that the name of his ex-fiancée had been flashing for several minutes. What the hell did she want? After all the chaos she had caused, with her offended prima donna scenes, what could it be now? After threatening him with a lawsuit that accused him of harming her public image, why did she want to talk to him? Damn it!

He didn't have any desire to hear her voice, and that reminded him once again how sterile and shallow their relationship had been. Alice Brown might be beautiful and sexy, but she definitely was not his idea of the woman he wanted by his side. How could he have tolerated her for the past six months? Perhaps people who thought that success had gone to his head weren't so wrong – being a very famous actor, wanted by movie directors and by women, must have confused him. It must have clouded his judgement and perspective. Wasn't he the one who used to dream of a *normal* life with a satisfying career, an intelligent wife, and a large family like his parents had? How could he have thought that an ambitious and spoiled actress like Alice would be the right woman for him? Of course he knew very well that the environment they lived in was not conducive to lasting relationships. Hollywood and the movie system were fascinating, brilliant, full of emotion and opportunities, but also full of predators – among them real vampires, thirsty for success, ready to do anything to get ahead.

At the beginning, Cade thought that having a woman by his side who could obviously understand the demands of being an actor, would have simplified his life. He was wrong. Alice had disproved this theory. After only three months it was clear that for her, their relationship had become a sort of competition for fame. Alice had just started to make her way into the movie system, while he had already been famous for four years. She thought that dating Cade would help her career, yet it wasn't easy to shine in the shadow of her famous and universally loved fiancé. So, once she understood that she wasn't getting the recognition she wanted, she found another way to get noticed: on national news!

The phone stopped ringing and he sighed with relief. The media war that Alice had instigated was dragging her down first. Her agent had probably advised her to come to some kind of agreement with him, to save face. But Cade had no intention of playing any more little games; he'd already taken part in this circus for too long. He never wanted to foster the juicy gossip that had emerged after their break-up, but he had been forced to respond to Alice's accusations and wasn't proud of it.

His own image had been damaged by all the stories in the press too, although not as badly. Moving away from LA had become necessary to let the events settle, to find a balance again, and put this disruption behind him. Yet, even hiding in this remote and unglamorous place wasn't enough. The text that he just received from Alice demonstrated this.

> I need to talk to you. This farce has lasted too long. Why don't we end it for good? No use running away. Come back and deal with me face to face!

"You would love to have more photo ops together, right? It won't happen, my dear…" he mumbled to himself, deleting the message. He called his secretary to have his number changed as soon as possible. He turned off the phone and collapsed on the couch.

His friend Philip's house was very different from his

mansion in Los Angeles. From the living room he could see every other room on the first floor, but it was spacious enough, furnished with taste, comfortable and peaceful. It was the ideal place to relax and off the radar. He hadn't been under siege for a few days now, there were no journalists in sight, and the refrigerator contained enough food for another week. This peaceful feeling was relatively new for Cade. As soon as he became famous, the opportunities to move freely around the States in privacy were almost non-existent. He had twenty-two rooms in his Californian home and enough money to travel to any place he wanted in the world. Yet freedom and privacy were still hard to come by. Wherever he went, he felt eyes on him and he saw journalists on every corner. If, at the beginning, the idea of becoming a star with a successful career had been exciting, now he began to weary of all the baggage that came with it.

He had felt an urgent need for a complete change of scene, and the pleasant, yet anonymous house in Staten Island seemed perfect for this purpose. It wasn't too far away from the lively social life of Manhattan, nor too central to be chaotic. It was the ideal hideaway to keep the journalists off his trail for a little while. They would look for him in Aspen, logically, since he often used to spend his winter holidays there. Even his crazy red-headed neighbor had pointed out that this wasn't a place for Hollywood stars! Nobody would find him here. Although… to stay locked in the house watching old movies wasn't exactly his idea of fun…

He decided to go for a walk. He put on a heavy coat, his woolly hat, and left. When he had first arrived by taxi, he had noticed a large park, a sign pointing to a museum, and a couple of stores that he wanted to check out. Suddenly, he was filled with fear at the thought of being recognized, but quickly pushed it away. The only alternative he had was to stay confined inside the house, and the very idea was enough to bring on claustrophobia.

As he stepped out into the wintry day, the icy air caught him by surprise. The temperature in New York was no higher than thirty-eight, and the weather report announced a further drop. It was weather that suited the holiday season perfectly, and in the Big Apple one could already breathe in the Christmas air. Cade wasn't accustomed to this temperature. Right now in Los Angeles it would be around seventy. He put his gloves on, turned up his coat collar and went down the stairs.

In the distance he heard cheerful music – lively notes and jingling bells – that made him smile. He wondered where it came from, but the loud, clanking noise of a pickup truck passing by distracted him. His eyes followed the truck. It was an old jalopy, its flatbed loaded with Christmas trees, being driven without any concern for the speed limit. The driver seemed unaware that his load was rocking dangerously back and forth, and of the voice shouting behind him: "Thanks a lot for your help and Merry Christmas, you fucking idiot!! I hope your trees fall out of your stupid truck! We don't need crazy bastards like you around here!"

Trying to restrain himself from laughing, Cade looked at the woman partially hidden by a potted Christmas tree she was trying to drag behind a gate. His outspoken neighbor seemed to be struggling. Curiously, Cade approached the small white house. He heard mumbling and cursing through the dense foliage. The curses were directed at the driver, who had apparently left the tree outside the gate, without helping her to bring it inside. Cade wondered if the truck driver drove off after some exchange with that eccentric girl. Three days earlier she had given him a hard time too. He hadn't forgotten.

Never before had he met a woman so unimpressed to find herself in front of a famous actor. Usually, people were excited and anxious to get an autograph or to take a selfie with him. On the contrary, his new neighbor had addressed him as if she rather looked down on him and his career and she had teased him mercilessly. On second thoughts, that truck driver did the right thing by leaving her to deal with the tree by herself!

But watching this wisp of a girl trying to drag an eight-foot spruce tree along her pathway, the gentleman in him suddenly sprang to life. Yes, she was arrogant, but still, she was a *damsel in distress*.

He went over to the gate. "May I help you?"

With a shocked yell the girl lost her balance and fell on her backside.

"Damn!" She mumbled.

Cade came around the Christmas tree and saw her. She looked comical, sitting in a flowerbed. She wore a giant sweatshirt, shapeless stained pants, and her hair was tied up on the top of her head. But he couldn't see her face because it was buried in the branches.

"Are you trying to hide?"

"Is it working?"

"Not really. Your hair color is too flashy to go unnoticed."

Sighing, the girl stood up. He noticed the light blush on her cheekbones for she wore no makeup. She was clearly embarrassed, but Cade could tell from her proud posture that she wasn't going to show any emotion openly. She stared at him with the big hazelnut eyes that he had already noticed on their first encounter – rather *collision* – and raised a mahogany eyebrow.

"Mr Star, to what do I owe this pleasure?"

Ignoring the sarcasm of *Mr Star*, Cade pointed to the spruce. "I was taking a walk, when I saw you struggling with this tree. I imagine you scared the delivery man away before he could help you bring it into the house... Am I right?"

"I did not make him flee, he was in a hurry! I was stuck in the attic and I couldn't get down quickly enough." She crossed her arms to protect herself from the piercing cold.

"Stuck in the attic?" Cade was perplexed.

"Yes! I suppose that in your billionaire mansion you don't have a cramped space where you put things that you hardly ever use, like Christmas decorations. And, if you do have it, I'm sure you have hired help who does the dirty job... unless you buy everything new each year."

"To be honest, I usually buy a ready decorated tree..."

"Ah! Just as I suspected. I'm sure that your life is so busy with social events, you don't have time for simple things, like decorating a Christmas tree," she said, returning to pull rather ineffectively at the big pot.

"Here..." Cade touched her arm, "Let me do it. Christmas will be over by the time you get your tree into the house!"

"It doesn't go into the house, but near the front door. I have all day to work on it. I can figure out." The girl attempted a protest, but Cade didn't give up.

"Let my *imposing physique* be of some use, besides making fragile girls stumble in the street." He flashed one of the smiles that usually made women sigh. Yet this particular woman seemed to be made of marble. Instead of giggling and melting, she limited herself to raising that eyebrow again. However, he must have confused her for a moment, because she didn't find anything to say. Cade took that moment of silence to move the tree to the indicated spot. "Is it ok here?"

"Slightly to the left… umm… no, it's better on the right. Wait, hold on – please push it more to the back…" Putting a finger to her full lips, she was considering his work with a critical eye, pacing back and forth. "No, perhaps it is better like it was before."

Exasperated, Cade stood up, "You've got to be kidding me?"

"Yes." She smiled, showing two pretty dimples.

Cade looked at her, feeling a curious vibration in his stomach. She was beautiful. He had noticed it the first time he met her, but this unexpected breezy smile had illuminated her face, making him forget her definitely shabby appearance.

Incredible, but true: he found this bizarre girl attractive.

Perhaps misunderstanding his silence, she offered an apology. "I'm sorry. Don't listen to what I say. I'm so plain-spoken, without filters. A hopeless case! These are only childish jokes; I didn't mean to offend you…"

"I'm not offended." He reassured her.

Suddenly a merry version of *Jingle Bell Rock* floated out into the air. Only then he realized that the music he heard was coming out of one of her open windows facing the courtyard. A small television was broadcasting Christmas music.

"Isn't it too early for Christmas songs and decorations?"

"It's *never* too early. December is here, and for me it's time to light up everything!"

"I understand. Do you want some help reaching the highest branches?"

She looked baffled. "Oh… Seriously? You really want to do this?"

"Why would I ask otherwise?"

"To be kind?"

"I'm not so kind." Cade took off his gloves and rubbed his hands. "It's been at least seven years since I have decorated a Christmas tree. It will be fun."

Her face brightened up. "Ok. I will go and get the decorations… be right back!"

While waiting, Cade began to open up the spruce's branches, the way his father taught him when he was a child. They must be well separated so there is enough space for any kind of decoration. He found himself whistling the cheerful

15

song that came from the television. Curious to say, but the idea of placing lights and glass balls on this tree really pleased him. It was one of the many *normal* things that he just didn't do any more. Also, being in the company of this girl was amusing – he couldn't explain why. This fun little diversion would help to chase away the boredom that had pushed him out of the house.

While he was taking off his scarf to free up his arms, he heard an all too familiar sentence.

"My god... I can't believe it!! You're Cade Harrison!"

Shit... Cade looked up to see a woman of about thirty-five-years old in front of him, staring at him with an open mouth. The irritation of being interrupted when he was doing something he liked, flashed in his eyes for a second, but he was quick to hide it. It was always a bad idea to turn a fan into an enemy, especially if the secrecy of his stay in Staten Island depended on *this* particular fan.

Giving her his legendary smile and casually running his fingers through his blonde hair, he said, "Well yes... you got me!"

"Oh my goodness, impossible! Cade Harrison in my neighborhood! May I hug you?"

Without waiting for his reply, the woman jumped into his arms, squeezing him with incredible enthusiasm. Ecstatic and giggling, she kissed him on both cheeks and began to search in her purse for a pen and a piece of paper.

"I need your autograph, Mr Harrison, I'm really an inveterate fan of yours... I have seen all of your films! Oh, by the way, my name is Martha... and let me tell you this, you're not only handsome, you're also a great actor!"

"That's very kind, Martha. Thank you!"

"Would it be too much, if I also asked for a photo with you?"

Cade shook his head. "Not at all, but can I ask something of you too? Can you swear to keep a secret?"

"Anything you want!"

"Great. Please promise me that you will not tell anyone about meeting me today. If the word got out, then journalists will come here and I will be forced to leave immediately." He gave a killer smile, hoping it would be more effective with her than it had with his neighbor... By the way, what the hell she was doing? Where was she? He was hoping she would save him.

Success! His blue eyes and his famous smile obtained the desired effect. His fan nodded, blushing with pleasure, and she solemnly promised that she wouldn't say anything to anybody until she was certain he was safely back in California. Cade let her pull out her cell phone for the usual photo op.

Finally, the woman seemed ready to leave. "It was a pleasure to meet you, Martha. Hope to see you again…"

"Oh, I hope so too! And don't worry about all those bad rumors… Alice Brown was not the right woman for you!"

Cade smiled, but didn't reply. He had already given her enough material for the tabloids to have fun, he didn't want to add anything.

When he was finally alone, he massaged his face. One day his jaw would stick by constantly smiling on command!

An applause made him turn towards the door. His neighbor was leaning on the doorjamb, holding a box of Christmas decorations. She seemed to be vaguely disheartened.

"Great performance! If I hadn't noticed your expression of terror at the idea of being recognized, I would have thought you were really flirting with that woman."

"I can't disappoint my fans…" he shrugged and sighed.

"Especially if you want something from them. This time you've secured the secrecy of your stay here, at least for a while. I'm sure that with slightly more effort, Martha Kendall would have allowed you to suck her blood!"

This was a reference to a small part he played in a vampire movie.

"I'm glad to know you've followed my career," he said, anxious to change the subject.

It wasn't the first time he had charmed a fan to get something he wanted, but for sure it was the first time he felt guilty about doing it. Damn!

"I go to the movies and sometimes I rent them." She said with a bittersweet little smile. Then she took the box over to the tree, without speaking or looking at him.

He felt her mood had changed and he became somber. What was the problem? Didn't she appreciate that he used his charm so that the woman swore to secrecy? He imagined she was probably happy somewhere with her photo, the autograph and a couple of smiles to remember. And he was free, hoping that Martha Kendall would resist mentioning that she had met him to friends and journalists… It wasn't the first, nor the last time he was going to use this method.

All of a sudden he asked, "Do you have a problem with me?"

She blinked, caught by surprise, "What do you mean?"

"I feel you use a disparaging tone every time you address me. Does it get on your nerves the fact that I'm famous? That I'm rich? Are you envious, or do you have some prejudice against my profession?"

Her cameo skin took a reddish tone. But it wasn't because of embarrassment. She was furious.

"I don't give a damn about your fame or your bank account. But maybe I have some prejudice about someone who's making a living using his image, and then complains when people recognize him! I don't trust anyone who's able to smile on command, just to achieve his goal. I don't know you, so I shouldn't judge, but I saw what you did with Mrs Kendall. Maybe I speak too much and out of turn, but I could never lie like that."

Cade shook his head. "It would be great if we could be ourselves all the time, but unfortunately for some of us this is not possible. I am an actor, acting is my work, yet the fame that comes with it isn't always pleasant, believe me."

Almost as if to confirm his words, they heard his name on the television and gave it their full attention. While they were arguing, the music program had been interrupted by the daily news, followed by a tabloid show that was giving an update on the Cade and Alice soap opera. The story had grown out of all proportion.

> The break-up between the Prince of Hollywood, Cade Harrison, and the TV Princess, Alice Brown, is continuing to make the news. Brown's agent has declared that Harrison has cowardly abandoned his fiancée and disappeared, just when she was trying to smooth things over and resolve their differences. A photograph, showing Brown very pale and tense, seems to confirm that she's really suffering for this apparently ended love. But what everybody is wondering now is what happened to the handsome soldier in *No Man's Land*. Is he really hiding from his fiancée and the media to defend his public image, or is he healing somewhere? The latter hypothesis seems improbable, given the harsh words Harrison used to describe Brown and her talent as an actress. Yet, we shouldn't forget the upset and stunned expression of the actor when Brown ditched him in front of millions of TV viewers…

Next the scene of Alice slapping his face in front of two

delighted anchormen appeared on the screen. The voiceover in the background questioned what really was the truth, and promised more sensational news to come.

Cade massaged his temples, feeling a migraine coming on. If that bitch didn't stop lying to the media, this story would go on forever! But he didn't want to appear too insensitive as he tried to silence Alice. She was still his ex-fiancée, a woman with a career, and he didn't want to destroy her. At the same time, he couldn't be passive and allow a bunch of ignorant people to call him a coward – people who weren't able to distinguish the truth from silly gossip.

All of a sudden he felt his neighbor staring at him. She looked perplexed. Was she judging him? Did she also believe that he was a monster who dismissed his ex-girlfriend's broken-hearted suffering?

"Do you have something to add to this pile of garbage?" He blurted out, coldly.

She shrugged. "Your way of ending a relationship is none of my business."

"In reality it shouldn't be anybody's business, but – as you can see – they don't understand that." He put his hands in his pockets. "Do you mind if I leave? I know I'd promised to help you, but…"

"No problem… you don't owe me anything. Thank you for helping me move the tree. Goodbye."

Cade nodded. His desire for taking a walk had completely vanished. He went back home and called his press office. He gave them a brief message to pass on to the media. Once he had done that, he collapsed into an armchair near the window. From that position he could see his red-headed neighbor decorating her giant tree. For a moment he envied her. It must be wonderful to feel carefree, to be able to whistle a silly Christmas song, while enjoying something as simple as decorating a spruce. He hadn't had anything like that for a long time.

People thought that being a celebrity opened every door, including the one to happiness. But it wasn't like that, at least not always.

Right now he could be in LA, dining in a great restaurant with friends, or relaxing in a luxury spa. He could be with his family and surrounded by love. However he was forced to go into hiding to find some peace – all alone, watching some perfectly unknown woman on the other side of the street his only diversion. In this moment Cade Harrison would happily trade his glamorous life with that of any average guy. Maybe even a guy that his neighbor would find worthy of a smile.

*

That day had started on a bad note. All her plans seemed to have gone up in smoke along with her carefree and cheerful mood.

Every first of December Clover set to work, full of enthusiasm, to make her home and her life more beautiful, more fun… at least for one month. The Christmas decorations – leafy garlands, scented wreaths and colorful lights – gave the rooms a joyful atmosphere that chased away the veil of melancholy for a while.

But in spite of her determination to see the positive side of things, she wasn't always able to look at life with a smile, especially when things went wrong. That would always dampen her enthusiasm.

Today the first source of irritation was that rude truck driver. It would have been really hard for her to drag the tree to the base of the stairs by herself, if her famous neighbor hadn't offered to help…

And then the second source of irritation… she definitely didn't want to admit that she might *need* a man! It was painful enough to remember – even for an instant – that she didn't have anybody who loved her, someone with whom to share dreams and fears, someone who wanted and was able to take care of her.

And now why all these gloomy thoughts? What about the man who set off this whole stream of consciousness?

She didn't know why exactly, but the Prince of Hollywood was able to bring out the worst in her. In his presence she felt uncomfortable, at a disadvantage and intimidated, so then she became obnoxious and aggressive.

Cade Harrison was simply *too much*. And not because he was rich or famous, but rather because of his amazing good looks and also because of his empathy, that emerged at random through the veneer of his otherwise controlled personality. Her

20

disappointment was still burning after the warmth she felt when he had offered to help her decorate the tree. Yet, she had to expect this change of heart from someone like him. Harrison seemed almost amused to help her and share this tiny, simple joy, and she felt happily surprised; but she had to return to reality. He probably just wanted to be kind and didn't really want to do it. It was possible that he always had to please people.

Then looking down at her disgusting clothes, she realized that she couldn't accuse him of anything. What man in his right mind wouldn't flee faced with such shabbiness?

"Maybe Mom isn't completely wrong. I'm not ready for Prince Charming!" She said to herself.

Actually, Nadia O'Brian didn't consider her to be totally hopeless. After all, this was her daughter and she couldn't turn against her own DNA. It was unthinkable! Yet she was convinced that Clover needed some help to become more attractive.

"Sweetie, are you sure you don't want to have a little bit of work done? These days big breasts are very fashionable, and also your lips could be fuller. You would be much sexier! Not to mention your clothes, Clover! You select such crazy colors and patterns… they clash with your hair and skin. You should dye your hair. Why not an ash blonde like mine, or a beautiful chestnut brown like your father? I'm afraid you have the bad luck of looking like your grandmother, love…"

"And what about my impulsive character, Mom?" Clover used to reply to this unsolicited advice.

"Unfortunately, there isn't any cosmetic surgery for that…" Nadia sighed, suddenly losing her enthusiasm.

Clover felt that the little interest her mother had shown for her disappointing daughter was dwindling over time… but she couldn't fake things and try to be someone she was not.

One thing that her mother seemed knowledgeable on was men's taste in women. For example, Cade Harrison's ex-fiancée represented to Nadia the ideal woman: the kind of beauty that would appeal to every man, even to a man who looked like a Greek god.

Yet she thought that the artificially perfect and sexy blonde must have had some invisible flaw – an insurmountable defect to deserve such public humiliation and coldness from her partner.

Although she wasn't usually interested in gossip, Clover had to confess that this time she had a morbid interest in hearing the latest news about the couple.

Was Cade Harrison really hiding from a woman? Was he a coward? It seemed incredible. She recalled his distressed and resigned expression, and the dead look in his eyes when he left.

She sighed. "Are you sorry for him?" A voice inside her asked, "After you insulted him, telling him he was a liar and a fake… now do you worry that he's suffering for love?"

Well, she wasn't exactly *worried*. The TV news had suddenly killed the enthusiasm she had seen in his eyes… and she thought that nobody deserved to have his day ruined by silly allegations… or by a broken heart.

But what she really missed was the chance to share the joy and magic of decorating the Christmas tree with someone. "Let me be clear, *whoever* was eager to share this simple joy would be fine!" A slightly less honest little voice inside her spoke this time.

Right, *eager*! She saw how he flirted with Martha Kendall – that guy was just eager to please. It didn't matter who it might be. She had to be rational. A famous actor like him for sure had more exciting things to do than decorating a Christmas tree. Honestly, she had to admit that Harrison certainly had other things to think about than spending an afternoon with a hostile neighbor! It didn't exactly ruin his day, and so of course he left.

She wondered if he really was suffering for his girlfriend. Seeing her – sad and pale – in that photograph, couldn't have been easy for him. Movie stars were capricious; every little argument between them found its way to the tabloids, yet maybe this couple still had feelings for each other.

Clover couldn't understand how Cade must be feeling at that moment. Her own past relationships had been unremarkable: not one of the guys she dated in the last ten years had remained in her memory. And rarely did she regret not having someone in her life.

She was probably a great romantic though. She would never be content with just any guy. She needed to feel powerful emotions, her heart racing and her legs shaking. Love should be like Christmas: magical and full of light and surprises.

Clover turned up the volume of the music to clear out her thoughts.

"Suck it up, honey! You will be lucky if at ninety you are still able to lose yourself with Christmas lights…" she mumbled, returning to decorate her tree, hanging golden glass balls on the highest branches.

3

"You will never guess who came to live in the house right across the street from me!" Clover said, when she was alone with her friends. "I've been so busy in these last few days, I almost forgot to tell you this."

"Who is it?" Zoe, always hungry for news and gossip, asked.

"Cade Harrison! But it's a secret. Don't let it slip, even under torture! If a journalist happened to appear in my neighborhood, Cade would immediately figure out that I betrayed him."

"Cade *who*?" Eric was perplexed.

"Cade Harrison, the Hollywood actor. Tall, blond, amazingly beautiful… he was in that film about the future, he was a soldier…"

"Oh, yes! That hunk!" Zoe leaned on the store's counter.

"Are you talking about the guy who signs his autograph on butts?" Eric sounded bored.

Clover smiled. "Exactly! Him! In fact, it was the first thing I told him. And he blushed, he was so embarrassed!"

"I'm surprised that *you*, you little nerd, didn't blush just talking about it!" Zoe said, pinching him on the cheek.

Eric adjusted his glasses on his nose. "I'm not a wan… an idiot!"

"Yes, *wanker*! And you could pronounce the whole word, without fearing to be struck by lightening…" Zoe blew him a kiss. "You're sweet, Eric. Always our little *Mr Perfect*…"

Eric walked away, mumbling, while Clover gave Zoe a withering look. "It's hard to believe he's still your friend after so many years of mocking him. Sometimes you're hateful."

"Eric knows that I love him. I just enjoy being a pest. Don't you love me too?" She giggled, flirting with her big gray eyes.

Clover sighed. "This strategy doesn't work with me, Zoe. Did you forget that I don't have a penis?"

Liberty Allen, the store's owner, entered the room at that

moment. As always, she was immaculate in her gray pantsuit, her blonde hair tied up in a perfect ponytail.

"Why do I hear you talking about the *male appendage* every time you're together?"

Clover laughed. "We weren't talking about that!"

"On the contrary! We were, and we were taking about a famous one… a golden one! I wonder if it is actually hard like gold…"

"Zoe!" Liberty and Clover shouted in unison.

Zoe ignored their shout. "Liberty, our wood nymph here has the good fortune of having as her neighbor, a man as beautiful as the devil!"

"I don't understand why the devil should be considered beautiful. It is a contradiction." Eric commented from his corner.

"However, it's just a temporary location for him. He's hiding from journalists and the media." Clover informed them.

"Ok, so he's a *temporary* neighbor, beautiful like a Greek god… do you know who he is, Lib?" Zoe was bursting with impatience.

"Well, considering that you find all men attractive who have massive muscles and small brains, it shouldn't be difficult for Liberty to understand who he is." Eric had a very sarcastic tone.

"It's Cade Harrison!" Zoe couldn't wait.

"*No Man's Land*, right?" Liberty asked, looking down at some files of recent orders.

Clover was giving some last touches to the Christmas window. "You know, Lib, you're incredible! You immediately remembered his most famous film, while Eric and I talked about gossip, and Zoe was thinking only of his physical attributes… you are light years ahead!"

"Well, it's not by chance that I'm the boss here. If the store were in Zoe's hands, we would have a men only clientele, with some special extra services maybe…"

"Yes, like in *The Client List*!" Zoe laughed. "But the women in that TV series happen to meet only handsome men, with amazing bodies! I don't think I would be as lucky…"

"And, on the other hand, if we had Eric as the store manager, we would always have an empty store, because of his shyness."

"Being someone of few words, who doesn't speak out of context, isn't necessarily the definition of shy." Eric protested.

"And, if we had *you* as a manager, Clover, all the merchandise would be broken or destroyed within one hour!" Liberty said, saving a little statue placed dangerously on the edge of a glass shelf.

"Sorry, *Mom*," Clover mumbled.

"Mom! I am just two years older than you… and thirty isn't old!"

Liberty looked at her, with an ironic smile, then handed her some papers.

"Here's your agenda for today. The first client will wait for you in front of Saks. He needs to find something original, as a gift for a couple that will marry on Christmas Day."

"Why do people decide to marry on Christmas Day? It doesn't make sense to me to combine two celebrations – one day less to celebrate!" Clover was protesting.

"I regret that I wasn't born on any kind of holiday. I would happily miss some of these damn celebrations!" Zoe didn't agree.

Clover grimaced at her. "Zoe, you're the usual *Grinch*! But I want to remind you that even *he* eventually recovered the Christmas spirit…"

"Well, no girl with funny hair has come to save me yet… and this year I will spend Christmas by myself again, since I don't have a boyfriend." Zoe came over to them, perfectly balanced on five-inch heels that made her sculpted legs look even more slender. "Christmas is a family and religious holiday. I don't observe traditions. I'm not the family type and I don't even go to church! Also, I'm too busy with work to enjoy the holiday spirit."

"Tell me about it! I not only have to look for gifts for relatives and friends, I must do it also for half of New York! You can add to this the terrible relationship I have with my family and my fluctuating faith, and you get the whole picture."

"Exactly! You too shouldn't go into such a frenzy during the holidays."

"But I adore Christmas! It's not only a holiday…"

When Eric turned on the colorful lights in the window, Clover brightened up. "See, Christmas is magical! Everything becomes glittering, vibrant, enchanting…"

"Jesus, Clover! It's also the busiest and most chaotic period of the year…" Zoe exploded. "You can see it yourself! Everyone is running around for weeks, searching for gifts that will be unwrapped and forgotten after ten minutes. Not to mention the hours spent cooking lunches and dinners that will make everyone fat for months."

"Yes, that is something I would happily avoid." Liberty mumbled. "The post holiday sense of guilt always makes me go jogging in Central Park – torture!"

"You can't convince me: I love Christmas!" Clover twirled under a branch of mistletoe hanging from the ceiling.

"Hmm, maybe we should take that down," Eric was pointing at the mistletoe branch. "I wouldn't want fanatic traditionalists forcing us to kiss them under the mistletoe."

"Clover, why don't you bring Cade Harrison to visit the store? I will wait for him right under the branch!" Zoe was giggling.

"I thought you just said you don't observe traditions…" Eric raised his eyebrows.

"Well, sometimes it's worth making an exception…"

"And sculpted biceps are worth it, right?"

"Yes!" Zoe laughed, giving him a pat on the ass. "Boy! It's very firm… congratulations!"

"He's blushing… poor Eric!" Clover came over to her friend.

"No, Eric! Look how your glasses get fogged…" Liberty joined the teasing.

Eric huffed, "I ask myself, more and more, why am I working with three unbearable women like you."

"Because your scientific stuff doesn't pay enough." Zoe smiled.

"And because, in spite of us three, your videos are selling well!" said Clover.

"You're more useful here than at NASA." Liberty handed a list to him. "Today you have two clients. First, a little family that will inundate you with pictures of children. They want a video that will be a gift for the grandparents. Then a young woman who wants a romantic video for her boyfriend. I suspect she will have a lot of material too."

Zoe nudged Eric. "You know how it works, right? When you get photos or videos from couples, you must show me everything…"

"Do you know the word *privacy*?"

"If you look at the material, I can do it too! We work together. I'm a business associate here, therefore I can decide to check on what the clients bring us – just to be sure everything is ok." Zoe laughed.

"You're a damn busy body, Zoe!" Liberty shook her head.

"Are you really thinking that clients bring us porno or sexy material to be put together for a Christmas video?" Eric sighed.

Zoe shook her dark bob. "What you may consider *too much*, can be absolutely normal for others. And anyway, sex is part of a couple's life. So why not? If I had to make a video about my best moments with a boyfriend, I would include…"

"Ok – I get it! If I get porno material, I will call you."

Zoe followed Eric with her eyes, "I adore this guy."

"We adore him too. So, please Zoe, leave him alone, otherwise one day he may end up resigning. Today you have to deal with two children, and then with the bridal couple, the friends of Clover's client. So, if you hear anything that could help her find the right gift, call her. Have a good work day, girls!"

As soon as Liberty left, Zoe stared at her list with all the appointments of the day, "I hate working with children. They can't sit still, not even for a moment!"

"Well, you can always cheer yourself up by inventing some hard sexy pose for the couple…" Clover replied.

Eric shouted from the other room. "Don't give her any ideas!"

Clover left the store giggling and began to walk briskly along Madison Avenue. She loved working there. It put her in a good mood.

Giftland was a two story shop that Liberty inherited and had managed for the last three years. Originally it was an old office supplies store that her maternal grandparents owned and ran for many years. Liberty had spent lots of summers there, helping them during school vacations. She still remembered with a certain nostalgia the smell of paper and old wooden floors. After graduation, she started to work there full time, bringing new ideas and helping them with improvements. The clientele began to become more eclectic, and eventually Liberty became the owner, after her grandparents retired. At that point she renovated the space and changed the sign. She worked hard to update the store's image, to make it more unique and trendy.

Zoe Mathison was her first employee. She was a talented young photographer looking for a job. Zoe was able to transform a simple photo shoot into something special; a great personalized gift for any kind of event. Liberty had immediately sensed her potential: her talent and her good looks attracted clientele.

Eric Morgan had arrived a few months later, to give to Zoe technical support. He created short films based upon various given themes. He was Zoe's friend from college, and – although they were incredibly different – they were very close. Zoe had strongly recommended him because of his conscientiousness, maturity and intelligence. He was discreet and shy, but he was indispensable in the store. There wasn't a client that he couldn't please with his work.

Liberty was not only the store manager, she also offered something unique to her clients. She wrote customized short poems, sometimes adding beautiful drawings. Clover liked to describe Liberty's work as a way *to capture those unique moments in time*. It wasn't easy to describe the intense emotions and memories of her clients on paper. Yet Lib could do it, in spite of her serious and staid attitude that made her look anything but romantic.

The typical client question, *what would you recommend as a gift for…* is what had brought Clover in. She was indispensable for this. She had worked for three years as a sales person at a mall in Maine, and when she had arrived in New York she was ready for a change. An unusual ad in The New York Times had led her directly to an interview with Liberty. Selecting the *perfect gift* was almost a vocation for Clover. She loved to see someone unwrapping a gift. She loved seeing the expression of surprise and joy when the gift was exactly right. For her it was an easy way to make people happy. She was intuitively able to understand dreams, tastes and expectations. She listened carefully to her clients and to their stories. She encouraged them to talk about the person for whom the gift was intended. It wasn't always easy to find exactly the right thing, especially when the people who asked for her help didn't have a clue… but she tried. There was always an important detail – hidden somewhere in a corner of their memory. Her task was to find it. Her ability to listen attentively was the secret.

But in her own life, even though she talked and talked a lot, no one seemed to pay much attention. They never really listened to her to know what she might like as a gift. In fact, she had started to make a *wish list* – a sort of letter to Santa Claus – to give to anybody who asked her, "What would you like for Christmas?"

Clover was crazy about surprises, and yet no one had figured this out. So, every year she sent an email to her mother with a couple of gift suggestions for both her and her brother. This way, she received *two gifts*, since her birthday also happened to be in December. Her brilliant strategy saved her from having to show fake smiles and to hide her disappointment in front of another anonymous and boring gift.

This gift problem was something that she would never let happen to her clients. She had promised this to herself ever since she started this job. That afternoon three people were waiting for her advice on how to make someone happy. One of them was a girl who hoped to impress her inattentive relatives with irresistible gifts. Clover was especially interested in this young woman, since she had found herself in a similar situation. Although, in her experience, not even the most compelling gift had conquered her mother and brother! She hoped her client might have better luck.

While waiting for the green light at a crossroad, she looked around with the same amazement she had felt the first time she had arrived in New York City. She loved its rhythm, the sounds, the variety of people and the immense skyscrapers looming over her. During the Christmas period, the level of chaos increased dramatically, yet Clover enjoyed this energy. It made her feel a part of something bigger, and she felt less lonely.

Shop windows were especially alluring: full of lights and colors, and so imaginative! She couldn't help but stop and look at them, even though her mission was to get in and out of the best shops in the city. But suddenly something else caught her attention. On the side of a bus that had stopped at a red light, she saw a large ad. Cade Harrison was staring at her: the gaze that took your breath away, his sculpted body able to provoke hot thoughts even in a convent girl, and that charismatic smile that could knock you down… Exactly the same effect his smile had on Mrs Kendall three days ago.

She recalled the episode in detail. She understood that someone like him had to be kind and charming – sometimes she had to do the same for work. Yet Mr Harrison had an exceptional talent. He was able to go from a serious, diffident and bored expression to a warm smile full of empathy in a second. That ability had to be one of his main strengths as an actor worthy of an Oscar nomination. But Clover found this characteristic repulsive! She had noticed his initial expression of irritation when Martha Kendall recognized him. Yet a moment later, he was making her swoon with his charm and kind words. He gave the impression that being in *that* place with *that* person was the best thing that could happen to him. Shit! He had almost fooled her too... how *could* you trust anyone like him?

Being by the side of a handsome and successful man had to be very challenging, but to be with someone who faked for a living had to be a nightmare! It wasn't surprising that most of the women abandoned by movie stars fell into depression.

The ex-fiancée of Harrison was a striking example of this. Beautiful, rich and famous, she was now crying bitter tears because he deluded her with love promises and then rejected her in front of millions of viewers.

After watching the talk show about the couple, she couldn't help looking for more news about them. What had emerged – among thousands of contradictory rumors on the web – was that after six months of an apparently harmonious relationship, Alice Brown had made a challenging move. She had asked him – on live TV – to marry her. Harrison practically fell off the face of the earth – he looked totally distraught. Then he stalled and asked if they could postpone the discussion for another time, preferably in private.

Clover could imagine that woman's humiliation at being so openly rejected... and in front of so many people!

Alice Brown had turned red with fury and began to accuse Harrison of deluding her all along. Then she stood up, slapped his face, and rushed out of the studio in tears. Cade was left shocked and embarrassed, but eventually he recovered some of his dignity. With elegance, he apologized to the delighted anchormen and the viewers, and then made his exit.

After this episode things between them went downhill. Alice Brown – because of a broken heart or because of pride and resentment – had started to give interviews in which she depicted Harrison as being the meanest of men. She described him as a cold and insensitive monster who had used her and then broken her heart, humiliating her in front of everybody, as if she counted for nothing.

Harrison had tried to answer with *no comment*, except for an interview that went viral: *This kind of argument should definitely remain private. But perhaps because of her lack of talent, Ms Brown has to use these inelegant strategies to get ahead and to obtain publicity.*

Predictably, Ms Brown didn't take this low blow well and the war between them went on, up to the point of forcing Cade Harrison to leave LA and hide somewhere. It certainly wasn't easy for him to defend himself from the journalists, yet to dismiss a love relationship so quickly was beneath him.

The light turned green, the bus moved ahead and Harrison's face disappeared.

Ah! *Men...* they could make you walk on air, and then – without any regrets – throw you aside like an old shoe, once they lost interest. It's better to keep away from them.

By the way, why was she wasting so much time thinking about Cade Harrison? It wasn't her business how he dealt with his relationships. She had to focus on her work. Today she should be more efficient and faster than usual. This evening was the best moment of the year: the giant Christmas tree at the Rockefeller Center would be lit! Her big priority right now was to finish everything she was committed to that day and be back home in time to get ready. She *had* to make it! She would never miss this event at any cost.

*

Tired of watching television as he lay on the sofa, Cade turned down the volume and picked up his cell phone. After dialling the familiar number, he waited to hear a friendly voice.

When he left LA, he had only focused on getting away from his problems and finding a way to relax. But now – after a whole week alone in this house – he began to get seriously bored. New York, of course, offered plenty of things to do, even more than Los Angeles, but the incredible cold was damping his enthusiasm. Also – even though Staten Island was a quiet neighborhood – the idea of being recognized had discouraged him from stepping out of the house. He had only to think of what had happened a few days earlier...

He had learned quickly how to enchant women. It was an easy way to secure favors – of any kind. So, on that occasion too, he had used his charm to *buy* the silence of that woman. He wasn't especially proud of it and couldn't forget the disapproving, nauseated expression of his neighbor. The thought of that little, outspoken, red-haired girl made him go over to the window, where he had a perfect view of her house on the other side of the street.

After their last turbulent encounter, he hadn't seen her again. Once he happened to gaze at her across the street, but she never even glanced in his direction. He was puzzled: usually women seemed to crave his attention, or at least they were curious... but this woman appeared to be completely indifferent to him, even simply as a man.

However, for some bizarre reason, Cade felt attracted to her. It wasn't something physical. She was pretty, maybe not strikingly so, and definitely not a classic beauty. The two times he had met her, she was bundled up in baggy clothes, so he couldn't really tell much about her shape, but certainly she couldn't be more than five-foot four and she was slender. Her face was the most attractive part of her. Her beautiful big hazel eyes, with hints of green, could shoot daggers at anyone; but the adorable dimples that appeared when she smiled, could change her expression in an instant. Her mass of flamboyant red, softly curled hair made her look like a woods nymph or a mischievous fairy. If his agent could see her, he would surely find a part for her in one of those fantasy movies so popular these days. But what had impressed him the most was her scent, which was of cinnamon cookies... an aroma that was good, sweet and reassuring. If she weren't so aggressively outspoken, it would have been a pleasure to be around her for that alone. Not that he was eager for female company! After the most recent events, the desire to have a woman by his side had definitely waned.

"Oh, my adored, *exiled* son! I'm so happy to hear from you..." His mother's voice brought him back to the present.

"Mother! It took an eternity for you to answer! I was almost ready to give up. Have you stopped staying glued to your cell, waiting for your favorite son's call?"

"Don't be so sure of yourself. You're not my favorite son any more... now Jake is the chosen son!"

"Jake! That wanker always hunching over his notebook, writing little romantic novels?" Cade joked, leaning on the window sill.

"His *little romantic novels* – as you call them – are bestsellers in the United States, and will be translated into four foreign languages soon! You're not the only celebrity among the Harrisons... rest assured, Cade!" His mother scolded him with affection – perceptible even at a distance. "Actually, Jake has become my favorite son because he has a great idea to save our Christmas."

"And what would that be?"

"His girlfriend Monique has a house in Brooklyn. Her parents are leaving for a vacation, so she invited Jake and all our family to spend Christmas there. So, since..."

"Since I'm in New York, it would be easier to join you all..."

"Exactly! It's not in the stars for a family to be separated at Christmas!"

"Mom, how much did it cost you to organize all this?"

"Love, you must be joking. I wouldn't spend a penny, even for something like Christmas!"

"Well, for sure you've manipulated Jake to push him in the right direction..."

"Your brother is so generous and sensitive! Otherwise how could he write such touching novels?"

"Ah! So now I begin to realize where I get my acting talent..."

"Surely not from that hermit, your father!" Grace Harrison mumbled.

"I guess he's not exactly enthusiastic about coming to New York..."

"He has started to complain about everything: about the cold that will destroy his poor bones, about jetlag... he suggested that – as rich as you are – you could have rented a private plane and come to see us."

"Well, I guess I could..."

"No, honey, I am very happy to have a change of scene. It will be fun seeing snow, and your sisters can't wait to go shopping on Fifth Avenue!"

34

"If you wanted to come to New York, I could have paid for travel expenses and your hotel anytime, Mom. You have only to ask. There isn't any pleasure in having so much money to spend, if I don't share it with you!" Cade's voice was now full of warmth and affection.

"You're wonderful…"

"Now am I your favorite son again?"

"You can't buy me with so little! We can pay for our airfare and hotel – you know this. But it will be more fun to share a house, and your father hates to spend money anyway. He thinks he has to save every penny, because he had to when he was young. So, Monique's house is the perfect solution."

"When will you arrive?"

"The morning of Christmas Eve and, knowing your father, he will want all day to recover from jetlag. So, we'll see you for dinner."

"Ok, Mom. Great!" At that moment something caught his attention – it was his neighbor who was heading home. He quickly said goodbye. "I will be talking to you in the next few days. Give my love to everybody!"

Clover was walking briskly, carrying several shopping bags. Her woolly hat was askew and her long scarf dangled dangerously between her legs. It was already dark and the streets were covered with a thin layer of ice. He had a bad feeling, even before he saw her slip on her front steps.

Without thinking, he grabbed his jacket and rushed out of the door. He didn't know whether he should laugh or be worried. This girl really had a hard time standing up!

He reached her in a flash and stopped at the gate. "Will I have the pleasure one of these days to see you standing firmly on your own two feet?" He joked with a hint of tenderness in his voice.

She was on her knees, worrying about the contents of her shopping bags. She looked up with those hazel eyes, before focusing again on her bags. "Hope is the last thing to die, they used to say."

He entered the gate, "May I help you?"

"Yes, maybe with a *survival course* for impossibly clumsy people! But first of all I need to check that nothing in my bags got broken."

"Perhaps you should check your knee first, it's bleeding."

35

She looked at her torn tights and at the scrape on her left knee, then she cursed in a whisper

Cade helped her up, saying, "Don't worry. I can pick up everything for you."

"Thanks…" she mumbled, climbing the steps, without taking her eyes off of him.

Feeling scrutinized, Cade gathered everything very carefully, then he followed her sweet smelling trail.

She opened the door and let him in. "You can leave everything on the sofa, thanks."

Cade obeyed and then he looked around. The house seen from the outside was in very bad shape, but the inside was better. She had old pieces of furniture, but it was neat and cozy. With some changes, it could be attractive. The first thing he would get rid of was her gnarled couch, it looked very uncomfortable. "Aren't you afraid you'll collapse in it and not be able to get up again?"

The girl followed his gaze, "I know, it looks pretty bad, but I'm fond of it. Everything here has the charm of the past – at least this what I tell myself, maybe just so as not to admit this place is a real dump! I'm waiting to be able to afford one of those modern, beautiful sectional sofas, maybe in a lavender color…"

"If you don't spend all your money on Christmas shopping, maybe…" Cade was pointing at the pile of bags.

"Oh – these aren't mine!" she said, taking off her coat. Underneath she wore a little black and red checked dress, heavy black tights and her usual tall boots. Cade finally could satisfy his curiosity. As he had imagined, she was delicate and slender. Yet she had seductive curves and full breasts. Her clothes didn't completely hide her figure. She had eccentric taste, especially in the colors she chose which were a challenge with that red hair… but the look suited her.

He watched her limping over to him, but felt a sense of disappointment when he realized that she was heading to the sofa, worried only about her precious purchases.

"You should take care of your knee, instead of messing around with those bags!" he said, almost irritated.

"I just need to check and be sure that everything is ok."

Cade was observing her every movement, until she finally sat down on the sofa with a sigh of relief.

"Are these your Christmas gifts?" he asked.

"Actually, they are gifts for people that I don't even know. I need to keep them here for a few days."

"Sorry, I don't follow you… Do you buy gifts for people you don't know?"

"It would be useless to explain this to someone who doesn't believe in Santa Claus!" she winked at him, smiling, and Cade felt confused by that sudden friendly expression. But he didn't have time to analyze his own reaction. Clover had turned to look at a clock hanging on the wall and said, "Damn it! It's very late! I have to go…"

She tried to stand up, but because of her knee and the antiquated couch this wasn't so simple. Cade took her hands and helped her.

"Your knee is still bleeding and your tights are torn. Where are you thinking of going looking like this?"

"To the Rockefeller Center. The Christmas tree will be lit tonight!"

"At least put a bandage on your knee and change your tights…"

"I can't! I might miss the ferry and be late." Clover protested, limping out of the room.

"There is a good chance you will be late anyway, looking at the way you are walking."

"You have no idea what people can overcome when they have a clear objective."

"And would your objective be to get an infection and risk hurting yourself seriously? Just to go to see a Christmas tree that will be there until January?"

"It's not just any tree, but *the Tree*! The lighting ceremony is a New York ritual. I can't miss it at any cost!"

"You have probably seen it already a million times."

"Ah! I see, you are *that kind* of person." she turned, looking at him with an almost nauseated expression.

"What do you mean?"

"A snob, insensitive to Christmas spirit!"

Cade didn't know what to answer. Honestly, he wasn't especially interested in these sorts of traditions, at least not since he had become an adult.

She continued with determination, "I'm not interested in the Christmas tree. What I don't want to miss is the moment when it lights up. Hundreds of people will be there, all enchanted, all looking up. The turning on of that switch signals the beginning of the best period of the year, when the city transforms itself and becomes magical."

"I assume you've never been to Las Vegas." Cade's tone was ironic.

"It isn't the same thing! However, I think maybe I would be completely dazzled, if I should ever go to Las Vegas." She checked the time again and her disappointment showed. "Shit, at this rate it's too late anyway."

"But it will certainly be broadcast live on TV." Cade said kindly.

She nodded in agreement. "Ok, I'll go disinfect myself and then turn on the TV. Thanks for your help…"

Seeing her so sad and downcast, Cade acted instinctively. He stepped in front of her and asked: "What time is the tree lighting?"

"At nine o clock, but to get to Rockefeller Plaza I need more than one hour, and the ferry leaves in less than twenty minutes. I had everything planned, minute by minute, but at this point I've already wasted too much time…"

"I bet we can make it by car. We have plenty of time." Seeing her looking both confused and hopeful, he added, "I can drive you there."

"You are very generous, but I can't accept…"

"I've never seen the lighting of the tree live and your passionate description makes me curious. Come with me." At this point he really wanted to go.

"Really? You haven't been there before! That's not good enough!"

"Well, help me fix it!" He laughed.

After a moment of silence, she nodded. "Ok! Believe me, you won't regret it."

Seeing her smile, Cade felt completely satisfied and returned her smile. Pointing at the clock, he said, "See you outside in ten minutes… or do you need more time?"

"I was ready to go with a ripped pair of tights; do you think I am the type who needs a lot of time to make herself beautiful?"

"I don't think you need it," he replied, sincerely. He was happy to see her confusion at this.

He headed to the door, and chuckled when he heard her

shouting, "Disguise yourself in a way that no one will recognize you! I don't want to be on the news tomorrow with someone signing autographs on half of New York's butts!"

He should have sued that crazy woman who had chased him on the streets of LA for that *intimate* autograph! He signed her ass just to get her out of the way as quickly as possible. He hadn't noticed the paparazzi nearby. Well, the story had really gone crazy in all the tabloids. His neighbor seemed to find it funny, and at this point he didn't give a damn about it!

Clover almost ripped her dress in her hurry to take it off. She ran to the bathroom for the quickest shower ever. No way did she have time to wash her hair… She put a band aid on her knee, cursing herself for another clumsy fall in front of the Prince of Hollywood, and went into the bedroom. She put on her lavender wool dress with funny embroidery that she always wore for the Christmas concert, and some lip-gloss. She brushed her hair and grabbed her coat. She was ready a few minutes early!

He showed up a minute later, and on seeing him again Clover felt her mouth go as dry as the Sahara Desert. He was fantastic: sexy as in *to die for* and elegant at the same time. She suddenly felt drab and insignificant. She thought of the many incredibly beautiful women he was used to seeing in California! She was sure he had never been out with a girl wearing a tacky dress embroidered with snowmen and limping like the Hunchback of Notre Dame before!

She should have worn something sexier to go out with a man like him. Wait – going out? She wasn't *going out* with Cade Harrison. He was only being charitable by driving her to the Rockefeller Center. He had probably felt sorry for her. That was all.

She stuffed the woolly hat into her pocket and wrapped herself up tightly in her coat to hide as much as possible. She kept her head up with the little dignity she had left.

But when he came over to her, with that irresistible smile, Clover forgot everything else.

"Right on time!" he said.

"Actually, I was ready a few minutes early, but I didn't want to rush you. I imagine that you need some time to maintain your movie star look…"

"Just enough to take a quick shower." he replied.

So, you're naturally gorgeous, Clover thought, following him to the garage, where a shiny black jeep was parked.

"May I at least know your name?"

"Clover O'Brian."

"Nice to meet you, Clover." Cade shook her hand. His hand was firm and warm. Incredibly warm.

Clover didn't say anything. She didn't even thank him for adjusting his pace to her slow limp. Yet, imperceptibly, something changed inside her. Suddenly, she didn't feel like she had a movie star by her side any more, but simply an attractive and true gentleman, willing to immerse himself in a sea of people, just to do her a favor out of kindness. She couldn't help being impressed. So she decided to behave as a polite and kind young lady should.

4

The Rockefeller Center was crowded beyond all expectation. The concert had started an hour earlier and it always attracted hordes of people – this year even more than usual.

In the past Clover was able to find a quiet corner to watch the show, but this time it was impossible.

Cade was looking around, surprised to see so many people, yet he seemed completely comfortable. Obviously he was used to being in large crowds. However, he tried very hard not to be noticed, and so did Clover.

"All the photographers are focused on the evening's celebrity guests. Mariah Carey, Rod Stewart and Billy Crystal are on the stage. They are more famous than you, right? You should be perfectly safe." Clover said to lighten up the situation.

"Of course!" Cade answered, without pointing out that they weren't exactly the trendiest of today's stars.

But Clover knew perfectly well that right now Cade Harrison attracted more curiosity than those has-beens. She wasn't indifferent to him either. The crush of the crowd kept pushing her closer to him. In this close proximity, she could inhale his scent, which began having a certain effect on her.

She wondered if these people might think they were a couple. Just for a few seconds she imagined that some paparazzi would take a picture of them together. The photo would appear on the latest news with the title, *Cade Harrison's new girlfriend?* This would raise hell, provoking millions of questions and a lot of envy. She imagined with a certain satisfaction her mother's surprise – her mother who thought that she couldn't attract any man on earth… God! It would be really fantastic!

These impossible daydreams, the music and the excitement she felt all around made her so happy. Not even her sore knee stopped her from darting around Rockefeller Plaza in search of the best spot.

She felt Cade's arm around her waist and her heart leapt in

41

her throat.

"Would you like to watch the show from above, away from this crowd?" he whispered in her ear. His warm breath on her neck gave her the sort of shivers she could barely remember.

Go ahead and shoot, fucking paparazzi. Right now! She thought, in a moment of total insanity.

She didn't know why she wanted to be photographed with him, to appear in a trashy tabloid tomorrow, but at that moment it was what she really wanted. When would it ever happen again, a stroll around New York with someone like him? She would frame any photo of them together, just to remind herself – in her darkest hours – that great things could happen and not only in fairy tales.

She tried to come back to reality. Damn! This guy had more talent than a snake charmer! Even if he didn't realize it.

What had he asked? 'Would you like to watch the show from above the square? She pointed to a little boy on his father's shoulders, and jokingly said, "Do you have something like that in mind?"

Cade was amused. "Not exactly, but if you prefer…"

"Well then, what's your idea?"

"There's a hotel nearby, with a perfect view of the square. We could get a room and watch the show from there."

"Can you really do that? Without booking in advance?"

"Hey! I'm Cade Harrison. I have more than just the privilege of signing autographs on butts!"

While Clover was laughing, he took her hand and led her away from the crowd. He was even careful about her sore knee! She followed him as though she were in a dream. She wasn't accustomed to having this kind of attention, especially not from a fantastic man, adored by everybody. Her sense of unreality was growing.

Her hand in his had become so hot, that she immediately understood why millions of American teenage girls had placed him at the top of the list of *the man of their dreams*. He was charismatic and sensual, but at the same time he had that nice guy look that conquered you. He was attentive and kind. It was only when he was embarrassed or under pressure in difficult situations, that one saw that cold movie star expression of disdain. It was difficult not to be won over by him.

The silence that welcomed them when they entered the hotel

caught Clover by surprise. It was strange after the deafening noise of the square. She looked around, admiring every elegant detail of the luxurious hall. She had never been in here before, but she had often dreamed of staying in a hotel like this, at least once in her life.

"I'll go and see if we can get a room… be right back." Cade invited her to sit in a comfortable armchair.

Mistaking his kindness for cautioun, Clover said, "Yes, I will behave, don't worry. I won't put on a show and ruin your reputation! Actually, let's establish a secret code so I can join you in the room without being noticed by anyone!"

"I just wanted to give your knee a rest!" With an exasperated sigh, Cade took her arm and led her over to the reception desk, behind which a man and a woman were talking quietly.

The woman immediately recognized Cade Harrison – Clover could see it from the hungry look she gave him. But the man seemed to know him too. He quickly came to attention and smiled warmly, saying: "Mr Harrison, such a pleasure to see you again!"

"Good evening, James." Cade shook the hand of the elegant concierge. "I know that I didn't book in advance, but I would like a room, if at all possible."

Both receptionists glanced at her in a discreet way, and Clover could feel herself stiffen.

What were they looking at? Were they finding it so strange that one of the most desired men in America was with a normal girl like her? Maybe they were just curious to check out the new prey… Clover began to feel uneasy and crossed her arms defensively.

"We'll check right away, sir, and see if we can help you." The receptionist looked at his computer screen. "How long are you planning to stay, Mr Harrison?"

"One hour, at the most."

The two receptionists tried to remain cool, in spite of their surprise. But after receiving the umpteenth curious glance from them, Clover elbowed Cade who tried not to laugh.

"Can you please clarify exactly why we are here, before they get the wrong idea?" she whispered. Then, addressing the concierge, she said, "You know, these celebrities! They are always at the center of attention in their public life, so they tend to be too secretive in their private life. Don't you think?"

Amused, Cade leaned on the reception counter, "My friend

and I would like to watch the lighting of the Christmas tree, but Rockefeller Plaza is too crowded for my taste… I don't want to be bothered by fans and paparazzi. Do you understand me, James?"

"Of course, Mr Harrison."

"We would like to enjoy the show from one of your best rooms. I will pay the full price, obviously."

"No problem. The room with the best view on the square is booked for tomorrow, so you can occupy it without any difficulty. My daughter is a great fan of yours. She would never forgive me if she knew I denied you anything!"

Cade smiled kindly and gave his credit card to the man. Everything seemed so easy when you were rich and famous. Clover was amazed by the fabulous suite with its warm tones of cream and gold and she was enchanted by the elegant furnishings.

"This room is the same size of the first floor of my house – but of course it's much more glamourous!"

"Yes, it's a beautiful space. Are you ok? I hope you didn't prefer to watch the tree lighting from the square…" Cade opened the curtains, exposing a large glass window.

The incredible view of the lighted skyscrapers left Clover breathless. She had lived in New York for several years now but she still couldn't get used to the sight of the city from above. And to watch the show from this elegant room, with a man like Cade Harrison, was almost too good to be true.

"Oh no – it's perfect!" she answered, coming over to him to open the window. The music and the choir of voices rose up and reached them. "Usually, I find a little corner in the square and cling to something, so this is definitely an improvement, Mr Prince."

"Is it so difficult to call me by my actual name?" Cade sighed, leaning on the window sill.

"I thought I might violate some kind of celebrities' ethical code… A prince and a common woman: such proximity could be dangerous. This room might be bugged…" Clover joked to mark time. Truthfully, she was dying to say his name out loud, but she was afraid of creating any sort of bond between them. Already, just a couple of kind gestures and engaging smiles made her dream crazy dreams… she didn't want to end up like those ridiculous women who buzzed around him like flies.

And besides, Cade Harrison wasn't for her. She should remember this! But when he smiled at her – just like he was smiling at this moment – all her good intentions went up in smoke.

"Clover, if there were any microphones hidden in this room, the small detail of your saying my name would be the least interesting thing imaginable for the paparazzi!"

Hearing this and seeing the image of Cade Harrison so close to a huge king size bed started to provoke erotic thoughts in Clover. She immediately chased them away, trying to focus instead on Cade's long fingers as he leaned out of the window. But it was a mistake. Her mind began to fantasize about the feeling of those fingers on her skin… and in a flash she imagined herself in the big bed with him – a consenting victim of passionate caresses and languid kisses. She felt a jolt of pleasure at the thought. *Damn it!*

She closed her eyes and concentrated on the music. Slowly the notes of *White Christmas* soothed her and reminded her why she was there.

"You've been so generous to treat me to all this. I don't think many people would have done this, especially for a crazy girl like me."

"It wasn't so difficult. Yes, you are different from the people I usually meet, but you're not so bad…" Cade looked at her warmly.

"I assume people bow and curtsey as *you* walk by…"

Cade shrugged. "Let's say they are all more… accommodating than you."

"So, they're all ass-kissers!"

He had a soft, low laugh and she felt another electrical charge through her body. She thought to herself, *he has a charm that slowly kills you… what a nice way to die.*

"As you obviously know, there is a downside to all this fame. Privacy is almost non-existent. Then there are the envious people, who are potentially very dangerous. You never know when people's affection is sincere. Do you think that the teenage girls that scream with joy on seeing me would do it if I were a simple mechanic?"

Clover pictured him in working clothes, dirty with grease and smelling of gasoline, and let out an involuntary moan. She was sure that women would adore him even covered with

45

motor oil!

She shook her head to clear out her thoughts. "Yes, I understand. Honestly, I always appreciate attention in my small intimate world; yet I couldn't stand such an invasion of my privacy. And I probably wouldn't trust anybody, if I were rich and famous."

She turned her back to the scene on the square and observed him, "Why did you decide to become an actor?"

"It wasn't exactly a deliberate choice. I went to a casting call almost for fun. I was with two friends who had taken an acting class at college with me. So, I began with getting small parts in TV series, then moved on to some more central roles in films. Four years ago I got the main part in a movie that has been very successful. And here I am. Celebrity has become an unstoppable avalanche. It's difficult to maintain any semblance of normality as a public figure, even though I try really hard."

"Have you ever regretted becoming an actor?"

"Not really. Every step I've taken – right or wrong – has led me to where I am today."

"But if you weren't so famous, you wouldn't have to hide…"

"True, but I wouldn't be here in New York with you to enjoy this Christmas tradition." Another dazzling smile.

Clover looked away to give herself time to calm down and return to normal.

"Considering how much you care about the Christmas spirit, I don't know if this is really a good thing or not!" she joked.

"Who knows? Maybe thanks to you, I will regain my childhood enthusiasm for the holidays."

Mariah Carey's voice suddenly attracted Clover's attention. Her eyes lit up as she sang along softly to *All I Want for Christmas*, swaying to the rhythm of one of her favorite holiday songs.

A few moments later Cade asked, "And what about you? While we were racing to get here, you inundated me with information about the giant tree, the lighting, and the history of this tradition. You didn't tell me anything about you. I only know your last name is O'Brian. Do you have Irish origins?"

"Yes, my grandfather was born in Ireland, but he moved to America when he was quite young. I've never visited Ireland, although I would love to. Do you have anything else you are curious about? I'm not such interesting subject, believe me."

"Sure, I'm full of curiosity…"

"Actually, I think my life is dull and boring compared to yours."

"You're kidding! I'm sure that you've had many interesting adventures with – how shall I say – your outspoken character!"

Clover laughed softly, shaking her head. "Frankly, my temper has only brought me lots of disappointments. Not everybody likes to deal with a hot-head like me…"

"Are you fishing for compliments?"

"Well, not exactly the kind of compliments *you're* used to getting… I'm just looking for some sincere admiration, not empty adulation…" Clover answered. "Actually, I *used to* look for it, but I gave up a long time ago!"

Cade didn't have time to reply, since the music and singing had stopped, and the countdown had begun.

"We are almost there!" Clover, full of excitement, took off her coat and threw it on the bed.

"Nice dress."

Shit! She had taken off her coat without even thinking. She had decided not to show her funky, unglamorous dress to Cade Harrison! She glanced at him, prepared to see a teasing look, but on the contrary, she saw only what she thought was *sincere admiration*.

With a sense of relief, she stared out of the window. "This is my personal tradition. I always wear this particular dress for the Christmas tree lighting. I know it's not a great dress and it's maybe a bit ridiculous, but I'm convinced it brings me good luck."

Cade interrupted her. "I just said that it's a beautiful dress. Why do you always have to read a negative hidden meaning in my words?"

"I guess it's an old habit. I grew up with lots of little ironic comments and jokes, so I've learned how to anticipate them… but now, don't talk! It starts in fifteen seconds!"

Cade came over and stood behind her. He placed his hands on the window sill and imprisoned her between his arms. "Do you have any other traditions we need to observe?" Now he was teasing her.

Of course he had moved to have a better view of the tree, but Clover was holding her breath, feeling him so close. "Yes!

usually I make a wish before the tree is lit, so let me concentrate."

Yet she was too distracted by the heat of his body to concentrate on anything. She tried to stay absolutely still. But when the crowd began to count the last five numbers in unison, she abandoned herself to the general excitement. She closed her eyes, felt Cade's warm scent enveloping her and instinctively made her secret wish.

I wish that at least once in my life a man like this would want me.

"Three, two, one… Wow!" Clover shouted, her eyes shining like a child's.

Cade was looking at her face instead of the tree. He found it much more interesting. He saw the myriad of lights reflected in Clover's eyes and could feel her genuine joy.

Honestly – when he had offered to drive her to Rockefeller Plaza he wasn't entranced by all those descriptions of the Christmas spirit, etc. etc. But now he began to feel the contagious excitement surrounding him.

When Clover turned and impulsively hugged him, he returned her embrace, as if he had known her forever.

She whispered, "Thank you."

"No, thank *you*!" he answered sincerely. It had been a long time since he had spent an evening like this.

Cade felt every curve of her delicate body through the soft fabric of her dress. What started as tenderness transformed itself into something different, something more intimate and sensual. Since their first encounter, he had admired the fine features of her face, her big expressive eyes and sweet dimples, yet he hadn't realized how much of a *woman* she was. Now her full breasts against his chest, that mass of silky hair brushing his cheek, and her spicy scent, provoked a series of perturbing thoughts. Her warm breath on his neck gave him shivers.

She must have felt his body's reaction, because she suddenly moved away. She turned back towards the window and said, "I'm sorry. This moment always moves me."

"Don't apologize… I was pretty moved too." he said in a slightly suggestive tone.

She seemed to want to laugh now, and Cade immediately relaxed. It was much easier to deal with her when she wasn't embarrassed.

He was so accustomed to women's sexual availability that he almost didn't feel emotions any more when in contact with a female body. But Clover had re-awakened his male instincts.

"Would you like to stay here for the rest of the concert?" he asked.

Clover looked at the square… "No, I think I've seen everything I wanted to. We can go now, although it's a pity to leave this room, after all the money you paid for it!"

"We could use it in a different way…" Cade, amused at Clover's suspicious look, added, "I'm beginning to feel hungry, and you?" he was looking deeply into her eyes.

Clover crossed her arms. "Actually, I do have an appetite, but for *food*." She made it very clear.

Cade laughed. "You immediately thought I meant something different. Naughty girl! I was thinking of room service…"

"There is a world out there celebrating, and you want to dine in a hotel room!" she avoided his eyes and grabbed her coat. "Let's go."

Cade, putting on his jacket, asked, "Where would you like to eat?"

"A hotdog at the first street stand would be perfect!"

"You go around the city with a filthy rich actor and you want a hotdog!" Cade didn't hide his surprise.

"Do you have something against hotdogs?"

"No, I adore them. And do you have something against filthy rich actors?"

"Well, even if I did adore them, I wouldn't want to take advantage of them…" she replied with an angelic smile.

Cade felt the impulse to kiss her, but he was – luckily? – stopped by the arrival of the elevator. He decided that keeping talking was probably the least dangerous thing he could do. Leaning his back on the elevator wall, he looked at her, "It's the first time I've met a woman who turns down a dinner in a luxury restaurant."

"I think you've probably never met one single woman who was able to deny you anything."

He gave her quizzical look. "So, is this the reason you don't want to have dinner with me? Just to be different?"

Clover opened her coat, revealing the embroidered snowmen on her dress and giggled. "I think I have distinguished myself enough. I don't need to show you anything more."

Cade felt touched and smiled sweetly. "Look, if it's because of your dress..."

"No, it's not because of my dress, nor am I trying to be polite. Really! It's just that expensive restaurants are not my style." She stepped out of the elevator. "However, if you really want to pay for my dinner, you can always pay for the hotdogs!" Her dimples suddenly re-appeared.

Cade didn't have time to reply, since the concierge came over to them eagerly. "Can I do anything else for you, Mr Harrison?"

"No, James. Thank you. You have been very helpful. You can tell your daughter I'm very pleased with the treatment you provided us... give her my best."

"You can do better than that!" Clover grabbed her cell phone and gently pushed Cade to the center of the hall. "Stay still. Look at me and smile."

"What are you doing?" Cade was puzzled.

"I'm sure James would be a big hit with his daughter, if she found a photo of you with your autograph under the Christmas tree. Isn't that true?" She addressed the perplexed concierge.

"Of course... Lisa would be very excited!"

"Smile, Cade," she whispered.

Hearing her pronounce his name gave him a thrill and he spontaneously smiled at her.

"Done!" Clover headed to the reception desk. "If you give me your cell number James, I can send you the picture. You should print and frame it. And then you can put Mr Harrison's autograph inside the frame." She took a pen and a small note pad out of her purse and handed it to Cade. "Come on and co-operate Mr Prince!"

"Why are you doing this?" Cade mumbled, signing the small paper.

"Actually, because this is my job." Clover sent the photo to the receptionist and handed her business card to him. "If you have any trouble finding the right frame for your daughter, come to Giftland. You'll find everything you need."

"I don't know how to thank you, Mr Harrison..." James said, while Cade handed him the autograph.

Cade glanced at Clover, saying, "It's not me you should

thank, James. I was just obeying orders."

"You've made my daughter happy, Miss!"

"I hope so!"

Once outside the hotel, Cade said, "So, you really buy gifts for people you don't know. It's your job – you weren't joking!"

"That's right – I'm a personal shopper. I give advice to my clients and help them find the perfect gift. It's what I do for a living, and I have to admit, I have a natural talent for it."

"Interesting. I imagine it would be very difficult to find a gift for someone like you. Who can possibly compete with Santa Claus?"

"Don't worry! Nobody seems to make the effort to find the appropriate gift for me," she replied a little sadly, shoving her hands in her pockets.

Cade noticed her woolly hat sticking out of one of her pockets; he put it on her head, his hands lingering for a brief moment on her soft red hair. "I'm sure your relatives and friends feel performance anxiety."

"I doubt it – I don't have big expectations. I just like to be surprised, but it rarely happens. And I find this bizarre. How can you not get hints about a person who talks freely about what's on her mind all the time?" Clover waved her hand as if to set the matter aside, and Cade had to quickly step back to avoid being hit. "Anyway, I'm very happy that I had that brilliant idea for the concierge's daughter! And, if James had even the slightest intention of telling anyone that he saw you at the hotel with a mysterious woman, we've bought his silence! Don't you think?"

"Wow! Clever girl…" Cade exclaimed, although in the past few hours he hadn't thought – not even for a second – about being recognized…

"A few hours in the company of a famous actor and I'm already thinking like a bodyguard!"

"And I wonder if – after an evening in your company – I should ask my mother to knit sweaters for me embroidered with Santa's sleigh!"

"Please, if this ever happens… call me!" Clover's happy laugh touched Cade deeply somehow.

*

When she saw her dumpy little house appear behind the bend, Clover let out a frustrated sigh. She knew that she wasn't Cinderella and that Cade wasn't a real Prince. She knew she wasn't sitting in a carriage that was about to become a pumpkin, but it felt exactly that way! The wonderful evening she had was coming to an end, and the thought that something like this would never happen again made her heart sink.

She couldn't ever imagine having such a good time. The lighting of the Christmas tree always left her in a euphoric state, but this year it had been much more than this… her memories of the evening would be unforgettable. Watching her favorite event in the company of a famous actor would already have been enough. But if the actor was also gorgeous, simpatico, sexy and kind, the intense emotions she experienced were hard to describe!

Exactly how many women could say they had walked the streets of New York eating hotdogs with a man like Cade Harrison by their side? Maybe more than she thought. Yet Clover had felt very special anyway, mostly because of the attentive way he treated her. Each and every one of his smiles was a cure for her melancholy side, which she seldom showed, preferring instead to wear her clumsy clown's mask. This man was able to penetrate her protective armor, yet – instead of feeling threatened – Clover felt serene and relaxed in his company. *Curious.*

Perhaps it was a big mistake to let down her guard with him like that. By the next day Cade probably would barely remember the hours they had spent together. And of course, at the end of the holidays he would return to California without hesitation. However, she would remember every single minute with bittersweet nostalgia.

When they were almost in front of her gate, she forced herself to look up with a normal, detached expression. She didn't want to show any of her feelings. Most of all, she didn't want him to know how much she was impressed by this evening. She wasn't used to receiving so much attention, so it really had been a fairy tale evening for her! She was sad because the day was now over. That was all.

"How is your knee?"

Clover sneaked a look at Cade's profile in the dark of the car. She shrugged, "I almost don't feel it any more, but I'm sure tomorrow I will have a big bruise."

"Put some ice on it. This is advice from someone who knows something about bruises."

"Please, tell me you are clumsy too and fall all the time, and you'll make me happy! Someone perfect like you must have at least *one* embarrassing flaw to give some balance to this unfair world!"

"Sorry to disappoint but no, I don't easily stumble, but at school I was the victim of two bullies. Now are you happy?"

"Very…" she giggled. "But I can imagine how envious they are now, having discovered that you have become a big star."

"Yes, in a way. It was my mother who took care of it. She had her revenge many years later, with my movie star success. Several times she had tried to stop those boys from bothering me, but without great success. She's stubborn, but she wouldn't hurt a fly. And she looks too innocent and fragile to intimidate anyone."

Cade's voice reflected the great affection he felt for her. Clover was touched, "Will you spend the Christmas holidays without your parents, or will you return to LA?"

"Actually, my mother has organized everything. They will all be in New York to be with me. She knows I need some peace after all that mess out there, and didn't want to force me to go back to California. Yet the idea of Christmas missing one family member is inconceivable for her, so here they come!"

"It must be beautiful to have such a close family."

Cade pulled into the garage and stopped, but didn't get out of the car. "Don't you have a close family?"

Clover tried to change the subject. "Did you see the sky? I think, – I hope – we'll have some snow soon."

"Good side step!"

"Listen, I don't have that much to say about my family. I have a few relatives, several nephews and nieces that I never see… in a few words: we don't really get along."

"So, will you spend Christmas all by yourself?"

Clover opened the car door and got out, seriously hoping he wouldn't ask her to join his family. She could enjoy his kindness, but she couldn't bear his compassion. So she lied.

"I'll be seeing them in a few days for my birthday. Then, they will invite me for Christmas Eve dinner, but I won't go. I'll have a much more fun dinner at a friend's house."

"So, it's your birthday soon?"

"Yes – in exactly a week."

Cade jumped out of the car to catch up with her. He took her arm to hold her. The asphalt was icy and slippery. At her perplexed glance, he shrugged and said, "You've already fallen three times. It would be good to prevent another fall."

"My self-esteem is grateful to you!" Then, in front of her door, she sighed deeply and added, "Thank you for the fantastic evening."

"It was a pleasure."

There was a moment of silence; they both seemed embarrassed. Clover had dreaded this moment, when they would have to part. She expected to see Cade disappear in the darkness of the garden path, but he was still there – waiting for her to go in the house.

Men and their gentlemen's conduct!

She opened the door, stepped in, and her heart skipped a beat when he called her name.

"Clover, will you have some time for me in the next few days?"

And when the hell wouldn't I ever have time for you! she thought.

"Hmm… yes, maybe. Why?"

"As I told you, my family will be coming to New York in a few weeks and I haven't even thought about their Christmas gifts. Would you help me find something special for them?"

Clover blinked – confused for a moment. "Oh, yes, I guess I could… but you still have plenty of time to shop – why do you need *my* help?"

"I'm not exactly sure I want to tell you how I solved my family's gifts for the last four years…"

"No – o – o! You mean you gave them money?"

"Well, you know, I'm always very busy."

"Bullshit!" Clover was leaning in the doorway, with her arms crossed. "Your kindness tonight almost fooled me… you're bad! To be busy is never a good excuse for not finding a special gift for our loved ones! It's what I love best about Christmas – it's the chance to make those we care about surprised and happy."

"My checks were pretty generous…" Cade still had that smirk.

Clover wasn't sure if she felt more like slapping him or kissing him. "Jesus! It's not the same thing, Cade! It's not a question of money, but of love."

"Thank god you aren't the person in charge of the economic destiny of the country!"

Clover sighed with resignation. "You're hopeless. Ok, I'll help you. Who do you have to buy gifts for?"

"Mom, dad, brother, sisters…"

"How many siblings do you have?"

"There are four of us, including me."

"Wow! Congratulations to Mr and Mrs Harrison…" Clover was wondering if they were all as attractive as Cade.

"So, when will you have time to help me?" He came up another step and a little closer.

Don't look at me like that… it's unfair! "What about Tuesday at three? Come to Giftland. I won't be very busy that afternoon, so I will be available…"

"Perfect!" Cade smiled, and Clover moved away quickly from this irresistible man.

"Goodnight." She stepped into the house.

"See you soon!" As he left, Clover was already dreaming about spending more time with him.

"Oh, shit! Clover, I'm afraid you're in trouble…" she mumbled to herself.

5

"Oh my god! I'm going to faint…" Zoe was emphatically fanning herself.

Eric looked up from the computer. "What's going on?"

"I think Cade Harrison – that Adonis! – has arrived early."

Eric stuck his head out of his office and immediately noticed the tall and handsome man in front of the shop door. "I think you're right, Zoe. He's well camouflaged, thanks to his winter clothes, but undoubtedly it's him."

"Think of the full impact he would have on women wearing his summer clothes, if he can be this sexy when he's bundled up like the abominable snowman!" Zoe sighed, looking in a mirror to fix her hair.

Eric looked at her, puzzled. "What are you doing?"

"Well, I'm going to ask him if he needs any help… so I can get a close look at him."

"Even if Clover didn't give us lots of detail, she has been really anxious, and kept repeating over and over again, that Harrison would come here today. This has to mean something!" Eric finished up on the computer and was ready to follow Zoe. He continued, "It must mean she feels something for him, so therefore, you'd better watch your step. Do you know what I'm saying?"

"Hey – it's not like I want him to ask me out. I'm just curious to see what kind of person he is, and anyway, until Clover gets here, someone has to take care of him, right?"

Even before she opened the door, Cade instinctively understood the girl wanted to check out the Hollywood actor.

"Hello," the girl said with an intense gaze and a well-modulated voice. "Don't stay outside. It's cold. Come on in, please."

"I have an appointment with Clover O'Brian."

"She's not back yet. She should be here any minute, but we can call her…" The girl leaned on the door of the office behind

56

her, "Eric, can you take care of finding Clover?"

"Already done. She's coming." Cade saw a guy with glasses coming into the room. He stopped to adjust some stuff on a shelf that didn't appear to need adjusting, and he hung around close by. Cade wondered if this guy was also checking out the famous actor, or his colleague, the brunette beauty.

"By the way, my name is Zoe Mathison, I am a friend of Clover's… nice to meet you, Mr Harrison!" The girl offered her hand, smiling at him.

Cade shook it, observing her. She was very attractive and aware of it. She seemed like a woman who knew what she wanted and how to get it. He wasn't a hundred percent sure if he was the object of her interest, for her attitude seemed ambiguous. She must confuse and delude many men with her seductive ways – a real *femme fatale.* Cade didn't know if this was intentional or not, but whatever the reason, the result was that she emanated a powerful sensuality.

However, this was one time in his life that he wasn't interested in getting too close to any woman. To be honest, he wasn't especially attracted to *this* woman, although most men would find her beautiful. Recently, he had begun to understand that there were other things about a woman that intrigued him.

He looked around the store with curiosity. Giftland was a two story shop packed with light, color, and a dizzying range of objects. One could find everything possible on shelves and display tables: frames, toys, small appliances, books, eccentric accessories, CDs, DVDs, all sorts of stuff. A big colorful sign behind the cashier described several custom services the store offered such as photo-books, video-stories, personalized little poems and of course, Clover's personal shopping service.

He had waited for this appointment with a certain trepidation. A few times he had felt the impulse to visit Clover, to knock on her door, but he assumed she was very busy with work. Most of all, he hadn't wanted to give her the impression that he was too eager to see her again. But actually he was. This was a new feeling for him and it made him wonder…

Of course he remembered what it was like when you started to warm to a girl, yet it hadn't happened to him for a long time. His last relationship, although it had lasted several months, hadn't made him happy – at least not happy like a child in front of a mountain of gifts under a Christmas tree. Yet this was exactly how he felt with Clover O'Brian. She must have cast a spell on him with all her talk of Christmas magic!

"So, I understand you're Clover's neighbor…" Zoe's voice woke him from his reverie.

"Yes, at least for a little while."

"I always thought celebrities spent their holidays in places more trendy and interesting than Staten Island."

"I spend most of my time in fashionable places, so – when I can – I prefer the *luxury* of returning to real life."

"Gosh, it's funny…" Zoe giggled. "You think you want to know a lot about movie stars, and have a gazillion questions to ask them; yet, when you find yourself standing right in front of one, flesh and blood, all of a sudden you don't know what to say."

"That's because everyone thinks of movie stars as being larger than life – sorry to disappoint you – but we are simply human beings." Cade put his hands in his pockets. "However, you should ask your friend Clover for a list of embarrassing questions for movie stars. She's pretty creative like that."

"Clover is unique," Zoe smiled. Her gray eyes were so intense they were almost unsettling. Cade didn't have time to wonder what this might mean. Just then, Clover opened the door and burst into the room like a tornado.

"Here I am!" She was breathless. Her woolly hat skewed, a scarf sticking out messily from one of her pockets and her cheeks pink and glowing.

Cade thought she was adorable. "I didn't want to rush you. Sorry…"

"Rush? Not at all. I just had to run to warm myself up. It's as cold as hell outside!" Then, grabbing Zoe's arm without too much ceremony, she said to Cade, "I'll be right back."

Once the two women disappeared behind a door, Cade found himself staring at the very serious Eric. He felt some empathy with him. "Are you the only man here?"

"How can you tell? Do I look that stressed?"

"A little bit!" Cade laughed. "I don't know about your third colleague, but if she is anything like the other two, you're in big trouble, dude."

"I would say that Liberty is actually the most normal of the three… that pretty much says it all!"

"Ah – is Zoe your girlfriend?"

Eric suddenly appeared guarded. "Why? Do you want to invite her out?"

"No. I only noticed the way you were sort of watching over her..."

"Zoe doesn't realize it, but she has the ability to provoke just about every man who comes into the store. She's a real flirt, so I have to keep close check on her."

He's crazy about her, Cade thought, and instinctively felt sympathy for him.

A woman entered the store and Eric went to help her. She looked at Cade with a lot of curiosity and he was afraid she would recognize him any minute. Thank god Clover came back.

"Shall we go now?"

"Yes, please! Get me out of here or I will be forced to sign an autograph – and I'm not sure *where* it will be!" He whispered in Clover's ear, burying his face in her hair.

Clover looked around and saw the woman staring at them. She grabbed his arm, leading him towards the door. "For god's sake! I certainly don't want to watch you branding cattle here in the middle of the store!"

Cade couldn't help but laugh.

Once outside, they started walking down Lincoln Street in silence. Cade noticed that Clover was still holding his arm; he hoped she wouldn't realize for a while. It was so relaxing to stroll along by her side – refreshingly *normal*. A girl and a guy, just like all the others, walking around New York City, shopping for Christmas.

"What were you doing at the store? You were there half an hour before our appointment."

"I was early, so I stopped by to see if you might already be there. I hope you don't mind..." Clover nodded and he continued, "I like your two colleagues, they're nice. But I didn't get a chance to meet Liberty and I'd like to..."

"Hmm... I don't think it's a good idea for you to come back to the store. It's a dangerous place!"

"Why? Because I could be discovered by some fans?"

"Well, yes, that too... but..." Clover looked at him carefully. "Did Zoe try to come on to you?"

"I really couldn't tell for sure. She does come across as being very seductive, but no, she did not flirt with me."

"I don't know how she does it!" Clover moved away and Cade immediately felt cold and empty.

"Does what?"

"To be so much a… *woman*! She's beautiful, intelligent and talented – in addition she's able to seduce any man who looks twice at her! It's definitely unfair."

"Yet you don't seem really hostile towards her."

"I can't even hate her! I just feel a healthy envy…"

Cade smiled at her frown. "You are two totally different women."

"Really?! Don't tell me… I can't help but notice it every time we pass in front of any reflective surface together!"

"No, no – I mean you are *both* attractive, but in a very different way. I'm sure you charm different kinds of men."

"Sure! I can seduce children and old men without any problem… sometimes even a father who thinks, hell knows why, that I would be a great mother."

"Maybe because you are sweet…" Cade brushed her hair from her face. He couldn't help touching her. "And judging from the way you played with those boys on Thanksgiving Day, you seem to have a great talent with children."

Clover made a face and continued her speech. "Zoe, on the contrary, attracts a larger range: sportsmen, musicians, wealthy WASP heirs and celebrities as well. In fact, you should fit perfectly in her men *category*…"

"It's not true that a man's *radar* always works the way you think. There are exceptions. Your co-worker is beautiful and she knows it. Maybe she exaggerates a little bit, relying mainly on her sex appeal to seduce men, but it looks like she's also able to attract *nice guys*."

"What do you mean? So, you like her too…"

"Wait a minute! I thought you had just put me in the *men with muscles-no brain* category! And now you say I'm the nice guy type!" Cade shrugged, "however, just for the record, I'm not interested in her. I was talking about Eric. I'm sure he has a major crush on her."

Clover stopped in her tracks. "How do you figure that out?"

"It reminded me of when I was sixteen. I had a crush on a cheerleader. I didn't dare approach her, but I was checking her out all the time. It pissed me off every time any other guy went near her. And Eric seemed very protective of Zoe."

"It's true. She doesn't suspect anything, but I have been able to tell for a while now. One day Eric opened up to me and asked me not say a word to anybody. He doesn't think he has a chance in hell with Zoe, so he tries to be content with things just the way they are. If she discovered the truth, he thinks it would ruin their friendship, and Eric would lose everything."

"It must be hard to suffer in silence like that, seeing her surrounded by potential boyfriends…"

"Eric consoles himself by watching Zoe's relationships fail even before they start. She doesn't have a very good taste in men… I'm afraid she's attracted more by physical assets than brains. She feels less threatened. Perhaps she thinks that an intelligent man couldn't love her…"

"Funny! Since she's adored by an obviously intelligent guy she sees every day!" Cade looked at her with a gaze of complicity.

Clover suddenly was curious: "What happened with your cheerleader?"

"She broke my heart by telling me I wasn't her type. Shortly after that she got pregnant and married an idiot… then she let herself go. She lost her looks and gained at least thirty pounds."

"Ha! It serves her right!" Clover laughed.

"I saw her again ten years later at a high school re-union. Of course, since I was becoming famous then, she immediately started to flirt with me."

"And?"

"She got a polite, but unmistakable rejection."

"Bravo!" She laughed with her adorable dimples and Cade felt once again the impulse to kiss her – right there, in the middle of the street.

Then she turned serious and asked, "What about your ex-fiancée in LA?"

Cade became tense – it happened every time he recalled the mess with Alice.

"Honestly, I think that our relationship started more out of boredom than a deep and lasting affection. In the beginning it seemed that we had a few things in common. At least we both had the same career that brought us together in an environment like Hollywood. But then I realized she was only using me and my fame to further her own career – to become known more as a star than as a mediocre actress."

"Well, it looks like she has succeeded with all the trouble she's been creating…" Clover observed.

"Yes, and I hope it will keep her warm at night!"

"So, you aren't suffering for her any more?"

"Suffering?" Cade shook his head. "You can only suffer when you still have feelings. This is not the case. Alice is definitely attractive, and at the beginning she was also somehow stimulating… but I soon understood that she didn't have any real love for me, beyond my movie star image. I probably just did what men do sometimes – I went with the flow – kind of passive, right? Now she has made me look ridiculous in front of half of America, and she's trying to play the victim with a broken heart. Too late, baby."

"Ha! She'll probably end up like your cheerleader, but even fatter and marrying an asshole!" Clover said, making him laugh.

"Too bad for the husband!"

"Ok, now to work. Who shall we start with?"

"My father. He's the hard one."

*

After about three hours, Clover felt that she had a complete history – down to the smallest details – of the Harrison family. They started with Cade's father, William. Clover learned about the loving relationship he had with his blonde and ethereal wife, Grace. She heard how Grace's abundant energy and determination helped to soften the rather sharp edges of her husband's difficult character. They had four children. Cade, who was the eldest; then Jake, now a successful writer; Heather, an interior designer, and Cecile, who was still in college.

Cade had talked at length about each one of them. He knew their personalities well, but – by the end of the afternoon – they still hadn't bought anything yet. Clover was surprised: he seemed to know his family's taste and desires, and in similar situations she would have already accomplished everything in a couple of hours.

"I thought it would be easy, but it looks like it's going to take me some more time and work to find the right thing for everyone in your family…" she said, while they were walking through Central Park.

"This time I really want their gifts to be special!" Cade walked head down. "But it felt like you had some very good ideas…"

"Apparently, not that many! We have been in so many shops and we're still empty-handed," Clover clarified. "You've moved away from giving them anonymous checks to being way too picky… nothing seems exactly right. You're a perfectionist!"

"Aha! Maybe it's your fault. You're the one who introduced me to the *joys* of Christmas, and now I'm obsessed with the idea of buying the right gifts." He put an arm around her shoulders, looking at her sweetly.

To avoid a panic attack, Clover slipped away and pointed at a café. "Would you like a *cup of heaven*?"

"I don't know… what is it?"

"You'll see."

The interior of the café was pleasantly warm, but Clover preferred to sit outdoors, on a protected terrace with a view of one of the lakes in Central Park.

"I always tell myself I should rent a boat and have a picnic on the lake; but I always end up here during the winter, when the lake is almost iced over!" Clover was sipping her hot chocolate with a pile of whipped cream on top.

"None of your boyfriends has ever brought you here for a romantic boat tour?"

Clover choked. "Pleeasee! Who would do something like that? If someone should propose it, I would immediately suspect a plot to commit a homicide. Drowning me in the lake could be a good way of making me shut me up."

"You pretend to be so tough! But I bet there is a sentimental romantic hiding under that crusty shell, and one day a man will ask you to marry him in one of those little boats, and our own little Clover will melt into a sea of tears, weeping with joy."

Oh Jesus! Don't encourage my craziness… she thought, trying not to picture the romantic scene. But it was too late. Clover already started to imagine herself in that situation. The vision was coming together: the silence broken only by the lapping sound of boats moving slowly through the water and the chirping of little birds in the air – a perfect background for the sweetest marriage proposal she could ever imagine. A man, blonde and beautiful like a Greek god, was leaning towards her, handing her a small velvet box containing the most beautiful diamond ring... a light breeze as the boat glided through the water towards the arch of a pretty little bridge covered by fragrant jasmine...

She made herself focus on her cup and changed the subject. "Hot chocolate, the best cure for every kind of pain!"

"After an afternoon with me, you really needed it, right?"

If I think that you'll leave and won't ever remember me, yes I need it, she thought. Better start stocking up lots of sugar.

But she answered, "In a way, yes... being successful at my job is one of my few certainties, and with you it didn't work. This hot chocolate helps to soothe me and accept the failure."

"There is no failure at all! I just wanted to think about it all a little longer... but I know I will end up following all of your suggestions. My father will be crazy about the complete *Star Trek* DVD collection with Leonard Nimoy's autograph... and the tickets for David Garrett's concert will absolutely thrill Cecile..."

"Yes, that could really be an unforgettable experience, especially if we could get her a pass for backstage. But we would probably need your movie star power and influence to do it, my dear."

"Of course! I will definitely do that for my little sister..."

"She's a lucky girl; she has a brother who can grant her wishes, like the genie from Aladdin's lamp!"

"It was your idea, not mine..."

"Yes, but you were wise to ask for my advice. My brother wouldn't ever do something like that for me," she said, with a shade of sadness in her voice.

"Oh, poor little lamb..."

"Very funny... but don't patronize me. I can still see you fretting over every idea that I dreamed up!" Clover mumbled, trying to ignore her inner desire to simply be hugged. The more Cade talked about his family, the more lonely she felt. She would have loved to be as valued by her family as he seemed to value each member of his.

"Hey, I wasn't rejecting any of your ideas, I'm simply a procrastinator. I'm sure we could still come up with brilliant new ideas before Christmas. So, you must give me some more time to convince me that these are the best gifts we can get..."

Cade stared at her with his deep blue eyes.

Damn! How could he do this? How can he make her feel in raptures with just a look? She didn't feel any different from all his stupid adoring fans, and she didn't like it. Clover put down her cup and suddenly stood up. "Let's go."

They walked in silence for a few minutes. Central Park was less cheerful after dusk. People were rushing to get home and there was a sense of melancholy in the air.

"Something wrong?" Cade asked.

"Not at all, but it's time to go…"

"You got up all of a sudden, and I thought that I had upset you by asking for another date."

"Another date? We didn't have a *date* today. I was just doing my job." Her voice was uncertain…

Cade put his hands in his pockets. "Ah, yes! I had forgotten. You would never go out with me for any other reason, because you despise my way of making a living."

"No, I don't despise it… I guess I just don't trust it… to trust someone who *acts* for a living is like putting a loaded gun in the hands of a child."

"My god! Do you think it's easy to be on the other side? It's difficult for me to trust too. It's difficult to understand who really cares about me and who is just interested in me as the famous actor."

"I'm sorry. I didn't want to be mean. After all you're a nice person and you deserve to be appreciated for who you are beyond your fame."

Cade seemed pleased. "Did I really hear a compliment coming from you?"

"Don't get used to this. I change my mind quickly!" Clover made a face.

"Yes! You have changed your opinion about me. I know you like me… I can tell… admit it!"

Clover didn't answer and diverted his attention by pointing at a souvenir stand. "Look! Snow globes…"

"You're avoiding my question, young lady."

"I used to collect them years ago. Every time I visited a place I came home with a new snow globe…"

Cade came over to her, but she moved away, towards the souvenir stand.

"Now that I think about it, I don't have one from

65

California."

"Ok then! I will send you one."

"In that case, I should return the favor…"

"Yes, you could do it by answering my question."

Clover looked at the snow globes, ignoring him. Suddenly she felt buoyant, like a young girl playing with the boy she liked. It was fun to leave him hanging.

She bought the snow globe that would best remind him of his days in New York. The metal base was engraved with the Manhattan skyline, and inside the globe the snow whirled around the Rockefeller Center Christmas tree. She handed it to him ceremonially with a great smile, "Here, for you. So when you're back in LA you will remember me."

"I couldn't forget you, even if I wanted to."

With her heart in her throat Clover turned and headed towards the park's exit. "You will be back in your city full of sun, palm trees and beautiful women… so, forgive my scepticism, but I don't think you'll remember these days for too long. I could pretend to believe it, just to please you…"

She couldn't finish her monologue. Cade had grabbed the two ends of her scarf to stop her and was pulling her towards him. She stepped back until she felt his chest against her. It was a good thing he couldn't see her face. She wasn't sure she could hide the powerful attraction she felt at this moment. She hoped that the noise of the traffic around them was enough to cover the loud beating of her heart.

Cade put an arm around her waist, pulling her even closer and they touched cheeks. "You should believe me, because I don't have any problem expressing what I feel… as opposed to someone who avoids difficult questions."

Clover wanted so badly to let her face feel the texture of his, but she didn't do it. She simply abandoned herself to the warmth of that closeness. The thought of being in the arms of a movie star, who was throwing caution to the wind to flirt with her in the middle of a public park, was overwhelmingly exciting.

"If I don't have an answer right away I will sell you out to the journalists as the cruel New Yorker who has rejected the Prince of Hollywood. They will persecute you and you won't have peace any more for a while!" He faked a menacing laugh and squeezed her tighter.

"This is a low blow!" She giggled, freeing herself from his hug. Finally, she looked at him with a solemn expression and affirmed, "Ok, if you need to reassure your ego... I like you enough, Harrison. After all, there are worse people than you around."

"That is a very cool way to give in, O'Brian!" He gave her a passing touch that suddenly became a warm caress. They looked each other in the eye for a very long minute. Clover felt the city disappear around them, but the magic spell broke too soon.

All of a sudden, the loud voices of passers by woke Cade from his reverie. He grabbed her arm and made to leave immediately. "Shit!" he whispered, accelerating.

"Why such a hurry? I think they've already recognized you, if that is what worries you." Clover sighed, trying to catch up with him.

"But they haven't had time to take photographs yet. You know, if the word spreads, we'll find ourselves chased by paparazzi in a minute. Frankly, I would like to avoid that." Cade waved to a taxi, quickly helped her in and gave his home address. With a sigh of relief, he leaned back on the seat. "You're too different from the women I usually see. I have never acted so recklessly before, like a school boy... and in the middle of the street! For a moment I had really forgotten who I am... and this behavior could become dangerous."

It was like a cold shower. Clover felt her enthusiasm die and her body go stiff. God! She felt so stupid. It was obvious that Cade didn't want to get photographed with a woman like her. She was *too different* from the women that he usually was seen with: she wasn't up to his high standards. He had a reputation to uphold.

For a moment she had forgotten that Cade Harrison was a Hollywood star... how could she forget something like that? He had played the latin lover with her, just to prove to himself that he could eventually conquer her, since she hadn't immediately fallen at his feet, like every other woman he met. But once he felt he had won her in spite of her reservations, fame overtook the man and he realized that he had to be more cautious.

A woman like Clover was definitely not enough for a man like him. That was the sad reality and she had to remember it.

6

Cade could tell something was wrong. Clover looked at him coldly. He couldn't figure out why. Suddenly she seemed like another person. What he had just said was more than he had intended, but he had spoken instinctively. He certainly didn't think his words would cause this kind of reaction.

"You're right," she said tersely. "I wouldn't want to appear in some trashy tabloid either, with some sort of caption. I prefer to remain *anonymous*."

"You've lost me, Clover," he looked at her. "Why are you so angry now?"

"Angry? Not at all. You're wrong – to get angry one has to be in an argument, and I'm not." Clover crossed her arms and stared out the window.

"What did I say to upset you?"

"Nothing."

"So, where did our friendly conversation go? I thought we understood each other…"

"It all went to hell when you started to curse and panic at the thought of being photographed with a woman *like me*!" She burst out, looking at him. Her icy eyes were furious now.

Cade was trying to follow her crazy reasoning, while she continued. "Let me refresh your memory. I was minding my own business, when you came up with the brilliant idea of asking for my help to find special gifts for your family. I accepted the job happily. I spent three hours of my day guiding you through New York's streets, even accepting the fact that you rejected most of my ideas! Then, all of a sudden you started flirting with me, fishing for compliments and reassurance, otherwise your ego – the size of Texas! – would go into withdrawal. And how does this fairy tale end? With us running like thieves, and of course it's my fault because I'm just *too normal* for you – this made you act like a school boy in the middle of the street, while the real Prince of Hollywood would obviously need someone who continually reminds him he's a famous movie star!"

Cade gave a worried glance at the driver, who was following the argument whilst looking in the rear view mirror.

Clover noticed it and almost shouted, "And now what? Are you wondering if the driver will sell you out to the journalists?" Then looking at the taxi driver, she asked, "You know who he is, right? Don't say you don't, because you may hurt his self-esteem!"

"Sure, I recognize him." The driver smiled, slightly embarrassed.

"Listen, please do me a favor. Don't spread around that you've seen *me* with him! I don't want to risk attracting the press. I'm a *normal* person, thank god! And just for the record, I am not his mistress, nor do I have any intention of becoming his mistress. I wouldn't ever want to ruin Mr Harrison's reputation."

"… ruin my reputation?! What the hell are you talking about?"

"Seriously, I get it. You need someone who reminds you all the time that you're Cade Harrison, right? I can try. Maybe I should ask you about all the Hollywood parties you go to… about Julia Roberts or Brad Pitt and Angelina Jolie… whatever!"

"Clover, are you crazy?" He grabbed her arm to stop her. "You didn't understand anything at all!" Cade didn't know if he should laugh or bang his head on the taxi window.

"Actually, I don't even have stupid questions about Hollywood's big stars. You're right, I'm *too different* from the people you hang out with…" She addressed the driver, who at that point seemed really amused. "Help me, please. What questions should I ask a famous, arrogant actor?"

"If they really kiss each other in the movie love scenes…" the driver said.

"Good question." She looked at Cade, inviting him to answer.

Cade restrained himself from laughing. "No, they are just what we call *cinematic* kisses."

What do you mean *cinematic*? Those are real lips, brushing, tasting, biting… you, movie stars kiss for real. I know you do!"

"Do you want me to show you the difference?" Actually, he

felt an irresistible impulse to kiss her.

She gave him a withering stare. "Don't even dare to…"

"Don't dare me…"

Clover tried to move away from him, squeezing herself against the taxi door. Then she addressed the driver again, "Do you have any more questions, sir?"

"Yeah – let's see. I could ask how many women he's had and how much money he makes… but I don't think it would be appropriate."

"I don't think you need the precise number of zeros to figure out how much money he makes just for *one* film. I assume the number of his lady friends isn't that much lower," she turned towards Cade, "did I guess right?"

"Ok. Do you really want to know?" All this furious drama had begun to amuse him.

"Ha, ha! Yes, of course! I already made myself ask idiotic questions about Hollywood, so for sure I don't also want to hear details about your sex life!"

The taxi driver seemed to like this idea of asking Cade questions, so he continued the conversation with him, while moving slowly through the traffic of New York's rush hour. Clover remained silent for the rest of the ride.

At times Cade looked at her profile, she was still stiff and unyielding. He really hadn't wanted to offend her. Actually, on the contrary, he thought it would make her happy by telling her that she made him forget who he was. But she had completely misunderstood and didn't seem to want any clarification. His heart felt heavy. He couldn't stand the idea that he might have hurt her feelings, even though it was unintentional.

Just a few minutes before they arrived at their destination, they passed a house overwhelmed by Christmas lights. The driver huffed and said, "I don't understand these people. They saved money all year to spend it on electricity at Christmas, just to have their home lit up like a landing strip!"

"You don't know how much I envy them." Clover looked at the illuminated house, enchanted. "I would do the same, if I had the chance. Right now I can only afford to put lights in my windows. I love to see them on when I come back in the evening; it's like being welcomed by a smile."

Her expression became wistful as they turned onto their street and she saw that all her windows were dark. "Well… it seems that my house is not in a smiling mood tonight."

Cade moved his hand to caress her cheek, but she moved abruptly away. He realized that he had spoiled an unforgettable, special day with one stupid sentence. He was afraid that it would be a while before he could regain her trust.

As soon as the car stopped at the sidewalk, Clover mumbled goodnight and got out.

"I'm sorry you had to witness all this drama," Cade said to the driver, giving him a generous tip. "I would be grateful if you could forget all this."

"No worries, my friend! It was one of the funniest things that's happened to me since I don't know when! I won't say a word about your private business, but let me give you some advice: hold on to that red-head. She's a keeper. She's the kind of woman who will never be boring. In your shoes, I would marry her right away!"

"Thanks! I will keep that in mind."

Cade saw Clover closing her gate, so feeling discouraged, he headed to his house. He felt there was no way of clearing up this mess – at least not that night. He had just gone in, when he heard loud thuds and cursing. He looked through the window at her house. What he saw gave him a feeling of tenderness and excitement.

After all, the evening was not over yet.

*

She heard him coming, even before she saw him at her gate. *That arrogant look on his face! Is he laughing at me?*

Sitting on the icy steps, chin resting in her hands, Clover gave him a nasty look, then returned to check out the scratch on her boot – she had made it by kicking the front door.

"What do you want? Haven't you seen enough of me today?"

"No – I haven't… what about you?"

"Frankly, yes. I want to remind you that your *perfect* face has been seen over and over again by millions of people, including me, and personally I find this quite boring!"

Her sarcastic tone didn't obtain the desired result. Cade lingered very calmly at the gate. "What's going on?"

"Nothing. Everything is fine."

"And when *everything is fine,* you kick your front door and sit outside on the steps in the cold?"

"Exactly. This is my way to recharge my batteries. After a shitty day like today, it's the best stress-reducer I know!" She looked up. "So that means you can go now. Thanks."

"Come on Clover, open this fucking gate!"

"Why should I?"

"If you let me in, I can explain it to you."

"You can talk. I can hear you very well from right here."

Clover knew she was acting like an obstinate child, yet she didn't want to be anywhere near him. The words he had spoken in that damn taxi still resonated in her head. She knew she had over reacted, and she was mostly upset with herself. She had let herself enjoy the ridiculous fantasy of being courted by a gorgeous actor. That had really made her feel attractive. How absurd! For Cade Harrison, flirting must be as natural as breathing. He did this all the time, both in his private life and on the screen. He was a professional at flirting! How could she have fallen into his net?

"Clover, it's freezing! If you don't want to open the gate, at least go inside…"

"You're so kind to worry about me, but I can't go inside my fucking house!" she mumbled, kicking the door again. "Stupid, old trash heap!"

"If you open this damn gate, I can try to help you…"

Clover stood up suddenly and came over to the gate, showing him a broken key. "Do you see this, Mr know-it-all? The other half is inside the lock. So, no, you can't help, unless you're an ex-locksmith with a new lock in your pocket!"

Cade took advantage of her proximity to wrap his arms around her waist. "Let me in."

"No!"

"You can't spend all night outside. You'll freeze!"

"I was born in December and cold is my element…"

"God, you're more stubborn than a mule." Cade exclaimed, holding her firmly in his arms. He lifted her head to force her to look at him. "Listen, you've misunderstood everything! I didn't think even for a moment that you could ruin my image or some other stupid bullshit like that! Only someone as nuts as you could dream that up!"

"Let's not start with my craziness. I'm not crazy! Although my mother would agree with you. She, too, is ashamed of being seen with me. She thinks I'm shabby, outspoken and lack class."

When he realized that he had at last worn down her resistance, Cade held her face gently in his hands. "I don't care about what your mother thinks. I'm telling you what *I* think. You're magnificent, Clover. Boisterous, stubborn... yes outspoken, but certainly unique."

Clover tried to step back, but Cade kept his hold on her. "Let me go..." She wanted to escape from that dangerous, irresistible man.

"Only when I'm finished." He was searching for her eyes. "When I told you that you make me forget who I am, I didn't mean to hurt you. Hell, it was a damn compliment! Do you have any idea how rarely I enjoy the luxury of feeling normal? I go around with the constant feeling of being followed, photographed... everybody waiting for my next *faux pas*. With you I've completely forgotten to look over my shoulder. Yes, this might create gossip, but this time you would also be at the center of it – everybody would want to know the identity of the *mystery woman* who made the Prince of Hollywood flirt like a school boy in the middle of a park full of people!"

"You weren't flirting..." Clover mumbled, escaping his eyes.

"You're right, not completely. But I am now!" he sighed, and pulled her closer to kiss her.

Clover held her breath. Cade's lips were warm and sweet. She felt the chill that enveloped her melt away. She couldn't move one single muscle. She remained still, the broken key clutched in one hand, and her woolly hat in the other. When his kiss became more insistent, she closed her eyes and her lips softened. She grasped the gate with one hand to hold herself up. Her head was spinning. Just one kiss and she was giving in... but how could anyone resist that seductive, persuasive man?

She felt overwhelmed. Just the warmth of his hands on her face sent waves of pleasure through her body. His smell deeply excited her senses, and her breathing became faster – interrupting the surreal silence of the street. It was the unique kind of silence that Clover knew very well...

Finally, she opened her eyes. Light snowflakes swirled

around them, visible in the glow of the street light. The atmosphere felt soft and quiet.

It was snowing!

Clover *adored* snow. Every year she waited with great expectation for the first magical snowfall. And it was happening right now, while Cade was kissing her! How could a romantic, dreamy girl not think this was a sign of destiny? It was all converging around her – she was helpless! Everything – Christmas, the chilly, electrifying weather, and the city itself with its special glow at this time of the year – all seemed determined to weaken her resolution. But in spite of his beautiful words and the magical atmosphere, she had to remember *who* was in front of her.

She stepped back, forcing herself to retain control. "Wow..." she mumbled.

He was looking at her in such a passionate way that her knees started to shake. He must have learned this on a movie set!

"Clover," he whispered, while touching her cheek with the tip of his finger.

She felt warm shivers along her spine, but she didn't give up. She couldn't allow herself to be taken in.

"A perfect scene, Harrison! You even didn't need a rehearsal... undoubtedly you're a great actor."

Cade dropped his arms and his expression became cold, but he didn't move.

Clover crossed her arms. Suddenly she was freezing. The only part of her body that was still warm was her lips, where Cade's taste still lingered. "What were you trying to prove?" she asked, a lump in her throat.

"Today would have ended exactly this way, if I hadn't realized that so many people were watching us. You would have appeared with me on local TV and tabloids, with stupid and embarrassing comments. But maybe that's what you wanted..."

"Not really."

"However, Clover, I can't erase who I am. The risk of being swallowed up by my professional life exists and it's not always pleasant. This is why I have to be careful, especially when I'm with people I care about. What I tried to tell you in the taxi is that I'm always on the alert when I'm with women. You're so different that I completely forgot about everything."

"Ok, I understand. I'm sorry if I over reacted. Let's forget it and not talk about it any more."

They looked at each other in silence for a few minutes, then Cade said, "Do you want to stay under the snow and get frozen to death?"

"I need to call a locksmith…"

"Well, if you stay here a little longer, your tongue will freeze. Hmm – maybe that's not such a bad thing."

Clover looked around with a helpless expression.

"You can stay at my house until they come to change the lock."

With some hesitation, Clover opened the gate. "I'm starting to think you bring me bad luck, Mr Prince. Since you've arrived I've fallen three times, my Christmas lights have burnt out and I've broken my key… not to mention my horrible performance in the taxi! I hope you gave a generous tip to the driver to buy his silence…"

"I asked him not to talk, and he agreed. Actually, I think he had a little crush on you."

"A crush – on me!"

"He told me you were a keeper – the kind of woman he would marry right away."

At last Clover smiled. "Great! I finally have a sweetheart… too bad he's already gone."

She followed him along the path to his house. Cade opened the door and let her in. "Go in, warm up and dry your hair. I will call the locksmith."

"Thanks – just use your movie star super power to have him to get here as soon as possible!"

Cade looked at her with an ironic expression. "Oh, so now my fame could be useful! And I want to remind you that if I hadn't insisted on bringing you in here, you still would be out there freezing and doing nothing!"

Clover clenched her fists. She had no intention of admitting he was right.

"So, what do you want me to do? Should I call saying who I am, to move heaven and earth to get a locksmith here, or should I call as a *normal* person?"

"The fewer people who know about you and my involvement with you, the better. So, this time you can forget about your super powers!" Clover left him and his triumphant smile in the hall to find somewhere to dry herself off. She tried not to think about how she had managed to put herself in such a precarious situation. Feeling so comfortable and at home with Cade was draining her resolve to keep a safe distance from him. She could still feel the taste of his kiss on her lips. Damn it! She could only hope that the locksmith would arrive soon. However, she was unable to fully convince herself that this was what she really wanted.

*

Cade hung up the phone with a satisfied sigh. He knew that he could get a locksmith in a few minutes by simply calling his secretary, yet he hadn't wanted to use this shortcut; and not only because Clover asked him not to. Now that the red-head was in his house, he didn't want to send her back home too soon. He had actually told the locksmith that there wasn't any urgency... he had won a couple of hours! Hopefully, he could use this time to bring back the smile of his... *his* what? Friend? Neighbor? Personal shopper?

He wasn't sure how to think of her. Did they have a relationship? It was a bizarre feeling for someone like him, who always used to have everything under control. In his world uncertainty could be a serious problem, and kissing Clover could be considered both an *uncertainty* and a *problem*. But he would do it again a thousand times!

He thought again of her soft, sweet lips and felt a wave of heat through his body. At first Clover had remained as still as a statue, while he sensed the world around him vanishing. But then – before she had stepped back – he felt her body melting, he felt her desire to abandon herself. The joy and excitement he had felt at that moment made his head spin.

God! If just a simple and innocent kiss had caused these sensations in him, he wondered what kissing her for real – passionately and deeply – would be like. He felt a rush of desire, but tried to restrain himself. If he wanted to regain her trust, he had to be careful. He shouldn't be in any hurry...

He found her sitting uncomfortably in the living room. She was staring at the empty fireplace. "What are you doing? Did you dry off?"

"It's not my house and I don't rummage around in a stranger's things."

"But I had given you permission…"

"Actually, this is not even really your house…"

Cade mumbled something under his breath. He felt a little discouraged as he started to build a fire.

Clover watched him with a cautious expression. "So, when is the locksmith getting here?"

"Not for a couple of hours."

"A couple of hours!" she suddenly stood up and began to pace the room nervously. "What the hell am I going to do for two hours? And if I hadn't allowed someone to let me into their house, I would still be outside freezing, waiting on my steps in the snow. What kind of service is that?"

"Well, you insisted that I didn't use my *star power* influence, so you have to be patient, stubborn girl!"

"No, I don't think so. I want to call him back – I'll make sure he listens to me!"

Cade grabbed her hand to stop her from making the call. "Why be in such a hurry? Don't you want to stay here with me?"

"No."

Cade tried to hide his disappointment. "Why? I thought you said I wasn't all that bad!"

"That was *before.*"

"Before what?"

"You know…"

"I thought we had cleared everything up; you even agreed that we were fine…"

Clover looked out the window. "Ok, but I really want to go home anyway. I'm cold and hungry. I've walked all day. I'm tired."

"Look, I started the fire, it will be nice and warm in a few minutes. We could have dinner here and then you can rest on the sofa. You can watch a film or read a book or a magazine… you can do whatever you want!"

She perked up and looked around. "Really? I can do what I want?"

"Absolutely, as long as you keep your cool… don't do anything reckless… and of course stay here, in the house." Cade was slightly suspicious about Clover's *plans.*

"Ok, first thing – I'm starving. Can you cook for me?"

At your service, *madame*."

Clover's mischievous smirk caught his attention.

"I'm beginning to feeling a bit nervous. What is it that you have in mind?"

Now she flashed a real smile with those adorable dimples he loved. "I saw some boxes in the garage, can I take them upstairs? No worries! I wouldn't *think* of doing anything dangerous. I promise."

"Ok. Do you need help?"

"No, I can take care of it by myself. You need to start cooking…"

Cade went to the kitchen to make something simple. He was thinking of her sudden mood swings. One had to pay close attention and know how to deal with her. When treated with kindness and tenderness, her bad mood suddenly lifted, her frown disappeared. In spite of her hot-blooded and stubborn character, she seemed unable to hold a grudge for very long. Behind the shield of that defensive attitude, she was very sweet. He instinctively sensed that she was incapable of real acts of spite and revenge. Nothing at all like Alice!

Thinking about his ex-fiancée, Cade realized he couldn't find one single memory of a moment when they might have shared any real closeness. They never had deep intimacy or cheerful complicity, not even real affection. In Alice's arms he had felt only brief moments of short-lived satisfaction.

On the contrary, just one single kiss with Clover and he was overwhelmed by powerful emotions. A few hours with her had given him more than his entire relationship with Alice had. In Clover's company, he had rediscovered feelings that he thought he had lost: the child-like giddiness of the holiday season, the excitement of the first snowfall, New York City so full of life… was he beginning to re-discover a sense of wonder?

Because of his fame and success, he had forgotten most of the things that really were important to him. Once he got back to LA, he wanted to put his life in order and modify his priorities. He wanted to be more available for the people whom he loved. He felt the desire to dust off old dreams and projects. He didn't want to get completely sucked into the vortex of his work and the social life that came with it any more.

But he knew it was going to be very sad and difficult to leave New York this time.

Half an hour later he joined Clover. Lost in his reveries and focused on the preparation of dinner, he hadn't worried about her. The light noise he heard coming from the living room had reassured him. She was still in there. He had no idea what Clover had found in his friend Philip's boxes, but undoubtedly it was something interesting enough to keep her busy.

As soon as he walked into the room, he couldn't help but smile. He should have suspected it. Clover was standing on a chair putting Christmas decorations around a window – garlands, glass spheres, small lights and random knick-knacks were all around.

The room looked different, more cheerful and lived-in. The candles she had lit gave it an enchanting glow. And that girl, standing on the chair, illuminated everything just with her presence.

He was damn close to losing his head for her!

This thought caught him by surprise. It was unnerving, but he couldn't chase it away. It had been ages since he had experienced any honest, deep feelings for a woman without even having touched her! He didn't know the exact moment he had started seeing her with different eyes – maybe that evening at Rockefeller Center. Whenever it was, his attraction for her had grown at incredible speed and was continuing to grow.

He came over to her. Impulsively he wanted to touch her body. He didn't know how, but he felt a powerful need to stroke her skin. He wanted to feel her warm and alive under his fingers. When he was within a few steps of her he observed her slender legs wrapped in tight black jeans and her well shaped butt. She wore a tiny orange sweater that had risen up, exposing a small, inviting part of her back, the color of milk.

Now he knew *how* he wanted to touch her…

"Stop where you are!" Clover said, raising her hands.

"Why? What's happening?"

"Do you respect traditions?"

He looked up at the mistletoe hanging above her head. "Absolutely! I respect traditions *very* much."

"In that case, don't move," she stepped down from the chair. "I wouldn't want you to come up with any crazy ideas…"

Cade chuckled. "Too late, honey. My thoughts have already taken that direction. Why did you hang up the mistletoe, if you really feared possible *repercussions*?"

"I had to use everything in the boxes! By the way, I didn't find that much... you don't even have a fake Christmas tree! Plus, I couldn't stand to see this room so bare!"

"If you think this isn't much, I can't even imagine what you did in your house!"

"Well, if that damn locksmith doesn't show up, you'll never know..." as she crossed her arms, Cade found his gaze drawn to her pretty breasts under the soft wool. *Hell – he couldn't think of anything else!*

"I hope you don't mind." Clover was saying...

"Mind?"

"... I've transformed your friend's house into a Christmas chaos!"

"If this makes you happy, I'm happy too."

"Please, don't be corny with me!" But her eyes were shining.

"Alright, I'll do my best." He offered his hand to her, saying, "Shall we eat?"

After a little bit of a struggle and some hesitation, she took his hand. Cade closed his palm around her slim fingers, enjoying the contact, and led her to the kitchen.

Clover didn't seem angry any more, but she still seemed cautious. That one single kiss had definitely changed things between them. It wasn't clear how, but the change was indisputable. Although he didn't have any intention of going back, he knew he had to proceed carefully. After all, he had no idea what thoughts might be spinning around inside her head. Maybe Clover was attracted to him... just maybe.

Yet, he could still feel the sting of her words accusing him of *acting* in real life. This had hurt him, even though he had heard it before. He wondered now if Clover's scepticism and lack of trust were insurmountable. He had kissed her simply out of desire, without thinking about it, and certainly with no ulterior motives. Honestly, he didn't know yet where these feelings would take him, but he didn't care too much about it. Enjoying his time with her and obtaining her trust were his priorities now.

After a quick dinner they came back to the living room, both feeling definitely more relaxed. To avoid any embarrassment, they had carefully avoided mentioning the kiss or even acknowledged the attraction they felt for each other. On one hand, the tension between them had eased, and on the other hand, it felt like their relationship had strengthened. And this made it difficult for both to accept that the evening was almost over – even though they didn't admit it. The locksmith would arrive at any moment.

Clover had noticed Cade checking his watch a few times. She wasn't sure how to interpret it. Was he eager to see her leave, or did he hope – as she did – to have a little more time to spend together?

In spite of all her resolutions, she couldn't help but feel herself shaking just by looking at him. It wasn't only that he was handsome. She had met very attractive guys before, but without feeling that she would melt under their gaze! Cade Harrison had something more: charisma, directness, and a kindness and attentiveness that especially touched her. He seemed to listen to her with sincere curiosity. Often he completely surprised her. A man like him could be with any woman in the world, yet he seemed to enjoy spending time with her.

Since they had that argument in the taxi, she noticed that he seemed more anxious around her. After their kiss out in the snow, he had begun looking at her more intensely, with a warm glow in his eyes. Was this desire? Now Clover was even more confused than ever.

At first she thought that his kiss was a way to flatter her, so she had accused him of *acting…* but the more she thought about the way he was looking at her all evening, and his smiles… the less she understood him.

Was Cade feeling something for her or did he just want to take her to bed? Not that she disliked the idea, but she wasn't keen on casual sex, and Cade was just passing through New York…

"What are you thinking?" Cade's voice brought her back. She stopped staring at the fire and turned towards him. He stood near the window with his arms crossed. He had taken off his sweater and he was in shirt sleeves and jeans. She tried not to look at his tanned neck, slightly exposed by his open shirt… but she couldn't help it… she kept thinking how much she wanted to feel its warmth and scent with her lips. Jesus! She realized she was staring at his neck like a silly teenager.

"What did you say?"

"You seemed to be concentrating on something. Actually, kind of worried about something, but now it looks like that concerned expression has disappeared."

Clover suddenly felt agitated. He looked at her like a lion, staring at its prey.

"I was thinking about work." she lied. "Tomorrow the most chaotic period of the year begins…"

"When do you think you will have some time for me? We should really finish shopping for my family's gifts, right?"

Of course she knew she would blow off all her appointments just to be with him. But she definitely couldn't say that. On the contrary, she had to try to put some distance between them. "Honestly, I don't know. The next few days will be very busy for me. Anyway, you already had several good ideas and you listened to my suggestions. I don't think you really need me."

"Ah! I get it. You're dumping me…" he faked carelessness, but Clover caught a deep disappointment in his eyes, before he turned towards the window.

Did he really wanted her to believe that he was sad about not spending more time with her? Whatever his purpose, she ended up feeling guilty. She wanted to go over to him and hug him so badly.

Hold on, Clover! She didn't know him at all. She must be careful. Cade Harrison was used to always getting everything he wanted. Maybe this was the only thing that intrigued him about her…

"Do you see how it's snowing? I haven't seen a snowfall like this in ages! In LA it never happens."

Clover moved closer to the window to watch the whirling tempest of snowflakes. "What a beautiful scene! Snow always radically changes the landscape. Everything becomes poetic, even the ugliest street is transformed by this blanket of white. Don't you…"

She couldn't continue. Cade's hands grasped her hips to turn her around and face him. "Sorry to interrupt you, but may I remind you of a tradition? We are under the mistletoe… if I don't kiss you immediately, I'll risk a year of bad luck." He touched her lips with his.

It wasn't just the very sweet kiss – Clover understood from his muffled voice, his gaze and the urgency of his touch, that Cade had waited all evening for this moment. This time he wouldn't accept a lukewarm participation or a rejection. He embraced her tightly and kissed her passionately. He challenged her... forcing Clover to abandon herself to his desire.

Suddenly she felt on fire. Their bodies clung together, a perfect fit. Hungry lips were exploring each other, their breathing had become almost frantic. She couldn't think any more. There was no way of going back. Cade's hands caressed her body, slowly from her hips up to her neck. When his fingers slipped under her sweater, she was breathless. The warmth of that intimate touch fogged her mind. She had only one single thought – to feel his body even closer to hers. She opened her mouth and put her arms round his neck. He began to move his hips into hers, slowly rocking them both, with a suggestive rhythm that made her moan. She felt a throbbing, powerful surge of desire between her legs. Their lips separated for a second to take a breath, then Cade started to kiss her neck, while his hand grasped her hair to pull her closer. Clover caressed his back and then, instinctively, she slipped her trembling fingers under his shirt, stroking his hot, smooth skin. The deep groan coming from his throat excited her even more.

And yet, somehow his passion and desire scared her – the way he looked at her was so intense that she was totally overwhelmed by her own emotions. She had never wanted anything that badly. She was afraid that she would never feel this way again, that her future would be probably without Cade. A future that was around the corner. He had a whole life that had nothing to do with her; he would be thousands of miles away, and he would be leaving soon. She was dreading the heart break she knew she would feel when he left for LA.

She turned away to avoid his lips. Cade felt the change and his hands anxiously grasped at her hips to hold her. At that moment they heard the sound of a pick-up truck. She thanked god as the truck stopped in front of the house, and she heard a door slam.

"The locksmith is here..." she mumbled, with a hint of uncertainty.

Cade looked out of the window, and she took the opportunity to move away. With shaking hands, she grabbed her coat. "Thanks for the dinner and the hospitality."

"You could stay until they finish..." Cade's eyes were still full of desire.

She shook her head. If she stayed there, in that house, for another minute, she would most certainly surrender to the

83

passion she felt. Then she knew she would have to pay a high price for a very long time.

"No, thank you." She felt protected by her coat. "I'm going now... goodnight." She ran out of the door.

Her heart, body and mind were fighting her resolution to run away from a magnificent man – the one man who wanted her and made her feel like no one had ever done before! Perhaps the people who considered her crazy, weren't so wrong... her mother would be pulling out her hair in frustration, if she knew!

Yes, she was still ambivalent, but her rational side had won. She repeated to herself over and over that she had made the wisest decision – to not get completely dragged into this dangerous game.

7

He had avoided it for too long, but they had to face it. Something was happening between them. Maybe he hadn't defined it yet, but it was powerful. He couldn't just sit there, doing nothing, waiting for her to understand and accept whatever this was.

He recognized and accepted his own feelings, and hoped that Clover could accept this reality too. He had already spent four days away from her, respecting her wishes; yet he had missed her deeply. He didn't want to push her. He had read her expression, and he saw a lot of fear in those large hazel eyes. The idea of scaring her made him nervous.

Somehow, he felt he understood her. Even though the desire to take her in his arms was intense, he knew he couldn't treat the whole situation lightly. It was complicated. He was heading straight into a hornet's nest – and he knew that feeling well. But he had never felt happier to run such a big risk in his entire life.

Today was Clover's birthday and he had no intention of staying away. He wanted to invite her out for dinner and enjoy her company. First of all though, he needed to be sure she was out of the house so the big surprise – her birthday gift – could be secretly delivered.

That morning Clover had gone to work, but he knew she would be back home in the afternoon. He had called the store and spoken to Eric. He knew that Clover would be home early to get ready for the birthday dinner with her family. Actually, this information was a bit of a cold shower for Cade. Now his plans for the evening seemed to have gone up in smoke, but he consoled himself at the thought of her big surprise when she saw the gift he had in store for her.

As soon as he saw that she was home, he put on his jacket and sped across the street now lined with big piles of snow. The cold was biting, but there was a beautiful sun; a bright moment before the expected snowfall that evening. It was exactly the kind of day Clover loved – everything was covered by a white blanket that glittered in the sun. Thinking of what Clover had said about her relationship with her family, he was afraid that her birthday might be spoiled. He didn't want that. He hoped to make her laugh with happiness.

He knocked on her door. No answer. He did it several times, then he grasped the knob and opened it. "Clover?" He heard noises and her curses coming from somewhere inside, and decided to enter. "Clover? It's Cade! Is everything okay?"

"Yes! No-o!! Ugh! This sucks!"

Her stressed voice made him chuckle. "Where are you?"

"In the kitchen – I'm struggling with this damn oven!"

As soon as he entered he saw the chaos. It looked as if a bomb had exploded in the middle of the kitchen. There was food everywhere, and Clover herself had flour on her nose and her t-shirt and jeans were stained with sauce. She stood in front of the oven. She had a pan in one hand that seemed filled with a sort of lasagna; and with the other hand – clenched into a fist – she was banging on the stove.

"Jesus! What happened?"

"There's no end to my shitty luck! It wasn't enough that I had the stupid idea to invite my crazy family for dinner, that I decided to cook for them and that they will be here in three hours… now this damn oven doesn't work! It really has complicated everything…"

Cade glanced at the counter top where there was flour all over the place and an egg yolk was dripping gently onto the floor. "Aha! Was it the oven's fault? Bad oven!" He tried to restrain himself from laughing.

Clover glared at him, furious, "Oh – so my troubles make you laugh, Mr Movie Star?"

"Honestly? A little bit!" He chuckled and came over to her, neatly avoiding a pool of sauce on the floor. He wanted to hug and kiss her, but instead he stroked her cheek lightly. "How can I help? What can I do?"

"Could you just prepare a dinner for three or four people in less than two hours and straighten up the mess in this kitchen in the remaining hour! That way I will have time to try and sort out my appearance. Although my mother doesn't expect class and perfection from *me* any more – she gave that up a long time ago – this mess could shock even her!"

"Why three *OR* four people?" Cade was perplexed.

Clover shrugged. "I don't know how much effort my brother made to convince his wife to come. I suspect this will be another year that she doesn't show up... but I never really know."

Cade nodded, staring at the pan she had in her hand. "Is that lasagna?"

"Yes, it should be. I watched a TV cooking program a week ago, and I decided to try this recipe." She was desolate as she stared at the mess around her. "But I'm not sure it was such a good idea."

"Do you have any alternatives?" Cade felt tenderness for her evident anxiety. She was biting her lips and frowning, but at his question she smiled. She looked at him, her eyes shining, "Pizza! A huge pizza with a mountain of French fries... maybe the French fries could spell out my name! I really thought about it, but my mother hates pizza. She finds it *so vulgar!*"

"I wonder why..." Cade was laughing.

"However, I'm afraid she'll have to make do with it, since my oven doesn't work and now I've lost all my enthusiasm for cooking."

"What about if I help you? I know how to cook. Nothing fancy, but something *more elegant* than pizza..."

Clover looked up at him, perplexed, and he noticed she was barefoot. Without heels she was five inches shorter, and had a touching, vulnerable air.

"Why are you here?" she asked.

"I wanted to wish you happy birthday..."

"That's very sweet. Thank you!"

"So, do you want my help or not? You can consider it my birthday gift..."

Clover sighed and nodded. "Ok, if you really don't have anything better to do..."

"I'm on vacation, actually *in exile* in a foreign land – do you remember? It's not much fun to be alone all day hidden in a house."

"Well, good then! Where should we start?"

"Let's start by going to my house. I have more kitchen utensils and ingredients there... also I can't work without my apron and my immaculate counter top!" He was very happy: he had just found the perfect excuse to get her out of the house.

Clover tried to protest, but he put a finger on her lips. "Shhh... come to my kitchen. Your oven doesn't even work! We will bring everything here when it's ready, and I'll help clean up this mess before your family gets here."

"Hmm... the journalists would pay a fortune to see you wearing an apron and mopping a floor. The Prince of Hollywood, *house boy for a day*!" she laughed.

Cade faked a terrified look. "I don't want to even think about it. The tabloids would go wild for months with this story!"

While Clover was putting on a pair of shoes and a jacket, he grabbed her keys with the excuse of helping her lock the door. He kept the keys and sent a text to his secretary, Scott, to go ahead with the plan to deliver Clover's gift to her house. He added some additional instructions. He had no doubts about Scott's efficiency. He was a clever guy and resourceful. He knew how to transform his thoughts into reality. Come to think of it, he should give him a raise!

Once they got to his kitchen, he showed Clover where everything was, and explained how to prepare some simple dishes. They stood side by side, enjoying the intimacy of cooking together. He left the kitchen just for a few minutes to give Clover's keys to the delivery people and to give them instructions. Half an hour later he got a text from Scott, saying that it was all done and that the keys were in the mail box. He sighed with satisfaction and went out to retrieve the precious keys...

Clover checked the time; her family were expected in less than an hour. "I should go clean up the kitchen and take a shower. The dinner will be definitely be beyond my mother's expectations; I don't want to give her any other reasons to complain!"

"Let me help you..." Cade was setting the dishes in the warming oven drawer.

"No, I can manage it. You already helped me a lot! And my mom and brother will be amazed by your delicious dishes... this is a great gift! Thanks again..."

"Not at all! I promised you full *service*..." Cade headed to the door and she couldn't help but follow him.

They crossed the street in silence. Cade began to feel nervous about his birthday gift. *What if she doesn't appreciate it?* After all, he had taken a big liberty with it. She was so proud and she might even get offended. His excitement about surprising her had quickly turned into anxiety, just as Clover was opening her front door.

Clover took off her jacket. "It's freezing in here. I need to turn the heat up higher. But there is a good smell… I remember the stink of eggs and of my horrible lasagna when we left. I was afraid it wouldn't go away, and my mother would notice something like that immediately. Sometimes she sounds like a snob, as if she were from a rich, aristocratic family; but the truth is she grew up eating hamburgers! Maybe *this* is the reason she's now…"

She couldn't finish her sentence as she stepped into the living room. Cade glanced at the new lavender corner sofa and the small glass coffee table in front of it. The room was different: more elegant, but still cheerful and informal, exactly as he had hoped… he looked at Clover.

She was completely puzzled. She kept staring at the room, as if she didn't recognize it.

"If you don't like it…" Cade passed his hand through his hair.

"How did you do it…?"

"Actually, getting you out of the house was easier than I expected."

"Oh, my god!" She went over to the sofa to touch the soft fabric. "It's exactly the way I wanted it! How did you know I wanted a sofa this color and with this shape?"

"You mentioned it, the first evening I came to your house."

"Really?" Clover's big eyes were glittering with joy and Cade began to relax. She seemed to be okay with it after all.

"I remembered you said that you dreamed of a lavender sofa… but I didn't remember anything else. I asked my sister for advice. You know, she's an interior designer. I described to her the size of your room, that it's not very large, and she took care of everything."

"Your sister has wonderful taste!" Clover turned round to sit on the sofa, then she had a second thought. "I will try it after my shower. I don't want to spoil it!"

"So, do you like it?"

"It's fantastic, gorgeous…" she stood in front of him. "How should I consider this?"

"As a birthday gift, naturally!"

Rising on tiptoes, she kissed his cheek. "Thank you, Cade. This is the best gift I've ever received." She smiled, her cheeks glowing with emotion. "And I hadn't even given you my wish list; you simply remembered what I said... I'm deeply moved and surprised."

"Isn't that the purpose of a gift? I learned from *my teacher...*"

"Jesus! First you helped me cook, then you've transformed my living room... now I can't really accept your help to clean the kitchen. I would feel too guilty!"

"I would also feel guilty if you had to clean the kitchen now, instead of taking a shower and relaxing on your new sofa before dinner."

Something in his tone made her suspicious. She ran to the kitchen, and seeing it neat and resplendent, she jumped with joy. "I *adore* you!"

Cade's satisfaction hit the roof. "I confess, I was a little nervous about all this. I was afraid you might have misinterpreted it, get angry for the intrusion, and throw all the dishes we cooked together at me! One never knows with you..."

"How did you organize all this?"

"Scott, my secretary – he can manage every detail, even from a great distance..."

"You should give him a raise!"

"Done!"

Clover looked around. "Well, now I only have to take a shower and get dressed."

"I'll bring the dinner over in a few minutes."

"You don't need to do that! You're not my personal waiter... I can do it."

"Ok, if you want..." Maybe this way he would have an excuse to see her again before her family arrived.

Clover stopped him at the door, "Cade?"

Yes?"

She seemed slightly embarrassed. "Would you like to stay for dinner?" She didn't even let him answer. Moving her hand as if dismissing her proposal, she added, "I know, it's a stupid idea! You don't even know my family – and it's probably just as well – also my mother would immediately go and tell all her friends that she met Cade Harrison, just to show off. Then you'll find yourself in trouble. I had forgotten you are incognito here. Please, forget what I just said."

Cade smiled and ignoring her torrent of words, said, "I would love to stay for dinner."

"I've proposed it because I felt bad letting you go home by yourself, after all the work you've done... but... wait... what did you just say... that you want to stay?" Clover blinked.

"Yes, after all my work this is the least you can do for me!" he joked.

"Look, my relatives are really boring... and I warn you: I will be very, very tense. Usually, I explode after ten minutes with them, although your presence might calm my mother and inhibit my brother... however, the possibility of an explosion still exists. It could be embarrassing."

Amused, he took her chin in his hand and said, "Now I'm starting to feel confused. So – do you want me to stay or not?"

She sighed deeply. "Yes. I really would like you stay and join us."

"In that case, I accept." He touched her lips. "I'll go make myself beautiful!"

"As if you really need to! You've already caused enough trouble in that department!" she mumbled.

*

Her birthday dinner always made her nervous, but this year she was especially anxious. She wondered how on earth she could have come up with the craziest idea of her entire life! Why did she invite Cade – *Cade Harrison!* – for dinner, and with her family?

Her mother would be totally shocked, definitely! It would be worth it just to see her jaw drop! But after tonight, Nadia O'Brian will want to be updated about Cade, every single day!

This had happened once before, when Clover was in college. For a while she dated the son of one of her mother's friends, and Nadia had stressed her with questions and advice the whole time they were dating. Eventually, when Clover left Simon, her mother couldn't stop patronizing and criticizing her... "you won't ever find another guy who can put up with your strange, difficult character! Darling, if you are waiting for Prince Charming you'll be alone for the rest of your life!" on and on *ad infinitum.*

Therefore, that evening Nadia O'Brian surely would make the *mistaken assumption* that there was something going on between Cade and Clover. So when he returned to LA she could only imagine her mother's reaction... "You should have thought about this *before* dating him... what did you expect? Of course he would be returning to LA!" ... *blah... blah... blah.* As if it wasn't already hard enough for her to think about Cade leaving!

Well, too late. She couldn't take his invitation back. She would have to explain to her mother that Cade was only passing through New York, that they were just friends and – more importantly – that she must not tell anyone that he was in Staten Island. She felt pretty confident about the latter. The idea of upsetting a celebrity would keep her quiet, although it was going to be hard for her not to brag to all her friends about the evening.

Trying to forget her anxiety, she focused on the difficult task of selecting what to wear. Her bed was covered with clothes! She had a nice dinner planned, a new elegant living room and a guest of honor to surprise her family, she couldn't spoil everything by wearing a flour sack!

She heard a soft knocking on her bedroom door and Cade's voice calling. "Just a minute!" She looked around at the mess. It looked like all her clothes had erupted out of her closet like a volcano! She was without makeup, her hair was soaking wet and she was wearing an old bath robe that barely covered her – a lovely image for the most desired man in the country!

"I thought you had to make yourself beautiful..." she tried to wrap the small bath robe around her as best she could.

"You told me not to overdo it, so it didn't take me long. I brought the food into the kitchen... Are you presentable?" Cade sounded amused, like he always seemed to be when she was in a difficult situation.

"Not sure about that..." She opened the door and felt breathless. He wore a black shirt with jeans. He had shaved, his blonde hair was still wet... and his extraordinary scent! – Damn it, he was irresistible! "Thank god you didn't overdo it," she mumbled.

Cade was smiling and staring at her, from her bare feet all the way up to her wet red hair. She felt shivers along her spine.

Hold on, Clover – you don't have time to jump on him!

"I don't know what to wear."

"I don't exactly dislike what you're wearing right now, but I'm not sure your mother would approve."

She laughed and moved towards her bed, to let him in. *I can say to future generations that I had Cade Harrison in my bedroom!*

"You seem to have lots of clothes here…"

"But nothing is right for the occasion, and it's your fault! If you hadn't helped me prepare a decent dinner and if you hadn't changed my living room – not to mention that you are the guest of honor – I wouldn't have to worry about what to wear. I would be in my filthy kitchen, wearing jeans and my *POUR ME ANOTHER GLASS I WANT TO GET DRUNK* t-shirt! Obviously my mother hates it, but it represents exactly how I feel when she visits me. I would have ordered that *inelegant* pizza and cut the evening with my family as short as possible. Then, I would call Zoe and Lib and convince them to take me out somewhere to get seriously drunk."

Cade didn't react. "Do you want me to leave? I can destroy the sofa, mess up the kitchen, bring the dinner back to my house and eat it by myself, if that's what you want."

His balanced reaction calmed her down. Clover sighed, "Okay, then please help me find something decent to wear."

Suddenly she found herself with Cade's arm around her waist. "At this time I don't want to help you get dressed, I would rather help you take off this kiddie robe," he whispered in her ear.

"What…?" She could barely breathe.

"Clover, I'm a nice guy, but if you keep bending over your bed with this tiny bath robe open, I'm not sure I can restrain myself much longer."

Her knees were shaking so much that she had to sit on the bed. She felt that her desire was as powerful as his. She tried to focus on her clothes again. She picked up something from the big pile and – twist of fate! – it was exactly the t-shirt she had described to him. "Here it is, my *suit of armor* for family reunions! It's a damn temptation…" She threw it to him and he caught it. On the back of the t-shirt there was a photograph of her that Zoe had taken: she was smiling at the bar of a pub, in front of a huge beer mug.

Cade laughed out loud, "It's fantastic!"

"Yes, I like it. It's Zoe's gift for my twenty-sixth birthday. Of course my mother hates it…"

"You should wear it, if you like it and it makes you feel comfortable… You don't have to impress anybody who doesn't respect your personality – including your mother."

She thought of her relationship with her mother, and the years of struggling to impress her, to win her affection and respect, apparently without any success. "You're right…"

"… and I don't think what's written on a funny t-shirt should be such a big embarrassment for the O'Brian family."

You must have some hidden flaw somewhere… she thought. God, it was becoming more difficult to resist the impulse of jumping on him and covering his body with kisses.

She finally opted for a pair of tight, sexy jeans and she picked out a close-fitting lavender sweater to wear underneath the infamous t-shirt. She looked up at Cade. His eyes were still full of desire.

"I have less than twenty minutes to get ready. Do you think you can resist your animal instincts or do you prefer waiting for me downstairs?"

When she saw his uncertain look, she threw a pillow at him, teasing, "Get out! I will be downstairs in a few minutes…"

She went into the bathroom and brushed her hair until it was soft and shiny. She carefully applied light makeup, some perfume, and finally got dressed.

Cade was in the living room, standing near the window, lost in thought. She wondered what he was thinking… it still seemed absolutely unbelievable to actually have Cade Harrison in her house!

"Whew! Now I have just five minutes to try my wonderful new sofa!"

He turned around to look at her, "Yes, tell me if it's comfortable…"

I would find it comfortable even it had nails instead of cushions, if only because it's your gift! she thought, sitting ceremoniously in the center of the couch.

"Mmmm… so soft… it's fantastic! You should try it too!"

Cade came over to sit next to her, and spread his arms on the backrest. "Definitely comfortable."

"It would be great if we could just be sitting here… doing

nothing."

"Really – *nothing*?" He touched her hair, gently stroking her head, and she closed her eyes.

When she opened them, she found he'd moved closer, his blue eyes were looking deeply into hers. He was caressing her face. He buried his nose in her neck, "You have a wonderful scent, Clover. It's one of the first things that I noticed about you…"

"The first thing?" She felt herself melting… "Are there any other things?"

"Several… your eyes are luminous and expressive, an amazing color… and your hair! I adore your hair, it makes me think sinful thoughts…"

"If you keep going, I'm not sure what's going to happen… my mother will be not only very surprised; she'll be totally shocked!"

"Do I have any chance of convincing you to come upstairs with me and pretend you're not home when your family arrives?" he whispered very close to her lips, while caressing her back.

She softly moaned… "more than one chance, actually."

Clover looked at that gorgeous man a few inches from her, his eyes lit with passion and desire. The temptation to forget rationality and wisdom and flee upstairs with him was overwhelming. But a sudden image of herself, sitting on this same sofa, and crying desperately after Cade left for LA, sobered her up.

She quickly changed her mind and moved away slightly. "It would be a very *bad* idea; a possible complication that we both should wisely avoid."

Cade sighed and didn't reply.

At the sound of the doorbell they both jumped up. "Here they are! Get ready to endure a very long and boring evening…" She went to open the door, hoping not to look like someone who had just spent the last few minutes indulging in *sinful thoughts*.

8

"Mom, Patrick! Welcome!" Clover exclaimed, putting on her best smile.

"Can't you do something about your icy walkway? I almost slipped and fell down out there! Thank goodness I held onto your brother's arm. I hate the snow!" It was the first sentence her mother said, coming into the house.

"I'm sorry, but the weather has the bad habit of not listening to me. It does whatever it wants: it makes snow, lowers the temperatures, and my path becomes iced. I don't know what to do any more with it!"

Her brother rolled his eyes. "Clover, why do you always have to be so irritable?"

"It's called sarcasm, little brother! I don't think many people around you use it, so obviously you don't get it…" Clover stood on tiptoe to receive a lukewarm kiss from her brother.

"Sienna couldn't come. Mathew has a fever, so she's staying at home with him. But she sends her love and best wishes…"

Every year her sister-in-law found an excuse to avoid her birthday dinner. It was just as she'd expected…

"Sweet! Thank her and send my love too! … *and you can also tell her she can fuck off, herself and her best wishes!*

Clover was wondering if Patrick could seriously believe his wife's excuses and bullshit. Probably pretending to believe her was the wisest thing he could do to avoid admitting he had made wrong choices and a mistake in marrying her.

"Oh, Clover! You're still wearing that stupid t-shirt! Are you doing it on purpose, just to get on my nerves?" her mother huffed.

"Mom, you offend me!" Clover emphatically placed a hand on her heart. "It's a tradition for my birthday party… and by the way, there's someone who finds my t-shirt very funny."

"I'm not surprised, given the kind of people you hang out

96

with… who said this? Let me guess, your insolent friend Zoe, or that morose boss of yours, or maybe your colleague Eric, that little nerd!"

Oh – the sweet taste of revenge! Clover thought, leading her mother towards the living room. "No, he's a new friend. You'll meet him tonight. He's joining us for dinner."

Clover was staring at her mother. She didn't want to miss one single detail of the scene.

"Good evening, Mrs O'Brian," Cade got up from the sofa.

Her mother's face became very pale and then suddenly blushed. She was a passionate reader of tabloids, so Clover didn't doubt that she would recognize him. But for sure Nadia O'Brian didn't expect to find an international movie star in the living room of her daughter, that loser! She was breathless.

Patrick seemed puzzled. He wasn't someone who read gossip, but he loved action movies, so for sure he had seen Cade Harrison's latest film.

"Mom, are you ok?" Clover asked in a modulated tone.

Nadia got over the shock and offered her hand to Cade. "Cade Harrison! What a delightful surprise…"

Cade smiled politely, shaking first her hand and then Patrick's. "I'm sorry to crash an intimate, family dinner…"

"Don't even think about it! It's an honor having you with us."

"Cade, as you can see we'll have enough food, even though you've joined us at the last minute. My sister-in-law couldn't come." Clover's voice was full of irony. While they were cooking, she had told Cade about her difficult relationship with Sienna.

"*Food*?" Patrick asked. "This is an extraordinary event for a dinner at my little sister's house!"

"A good attempt at sarcasm… Bravo! See, even *you* can learn…"

For a few minutes there was an embarrassing silence in the room, until Clover said, "I don't know about you, but I'm starving! Shall we go to eat?"

"Perhaps you should serve an aperitif in the living room before dinner…" her mother observed, then she whispered to her, "You have a famous actor here, try to behave with some class, please!"

While Clover restrained herself from doing backflips to

embarrass her mother even more, Cade rescued her, saying, "I think eating now is a great idea. Your daughter has cooked all afternoon. There is such a delicious smell, I can't wait to taste what she's made!"

Oh my god! Marry me! Clover thought – it was wonderful to have such an ally...

"Did you cook?" Patrick faked admiration. "I hope you have an effective antacid to give me after dinner."

"Ha – ha! Really, little brother – very funny! Apparently being with me brings back your sense of irony..."

Their mother was staring at them with a severe and disapproving look, like when they were naughty children.

"I didn't know that my daughter knew you. She never told me." She addressed Cade.

"I don't think she has had time to mention it... and I specifically asked her not to spread the word. I'm in New York incognito."

"Oh, of course! I understand perfectly. Sometimes the show business environment can be so very stressful!"

"Are you in show business too?"

Clover pretended to throw up behind her brother's back, and Cade coughed to hide a laugh.

"My image has appeared in some ad campaign for beauty products. Nothing compared to your fame, Mr Harrison – of course!"

"Please, call me Cade."

"It would be an honor!"

"If you keep talking to her, she'll have an orgasm at the dinner table. I would rather prefer to avoid that scene..." Clover whispered in Cade's ear.

"How did you meet each other?" Patrick asked, as they sat at the dinner table. The question seemed to show a sincere interest and that surprised Clover. Her brother used to be very protective of her, but after he got married he had become completely disinterested.

"A friend talked to me about Giftland's services and Clover helped me select my Christmas gifts." Cade lied.

"That's lovely... I hope my daughter had some good advice for you!"

"Absolutely. She has wonderful ideas, unique taste, and a really contagious Christmas spirit." He glanced at Clover, smiling. "It has been a long time since I've enjoyed myself so much. Your daughter is very nice and original; but I don't know why I'm saying this to you. You're her mother and I'm sure you know this very well!"

Her mother almost choked on a sip of white wine, and Clover was ready to swear eternal gratitude to Cade!

The dinner went on without any major crises, actually better than Clover had expected. Yet she kept checking the time, hoping it would be over soon. In spite of Cade's presence – which had restrained her mother and intimidated her brother – the cutting remarks and the usual critical attitude weren't lacking all evening. Also, she couldn't stand her mother's *kissing ass* attitude with Cade. She almost came on to him – it had been frankly embarrassing. She was old enough to be his mother!

Most of all, her own presence became totally irrelevant. She didn't have a chance to talk. The O'Brian widow monopolized the evening, while her brother had remained mostly silent. Clover found herself carrying plates back and forth to the kitchen like a maid.

Her birthday party?! Fuck! They didn't even wish her happy birthday. Her mother, as always, had brought some banal cookies. Forget a cake with candles!

She barely touched the food, but she drank a lot of wine – although she didn't feel as drunk as she had hoped.

"Clover, aren't you hungry? You hardly ate a thing…" at least Cade had noticed. She shrugged.

"How long will you be staying in New York?" Nadia asked.

"Not very long," Cade answered laconically.

"Would anyone like dessert?" Clover was heading to the kitchen.

Her mother ignored her and kept on talking to Cade. "It was such a pleasure meeting you. You have made a huge difference to our evening – really quite unexpected!"

Thank you, Mom! "So – do you all want dessert or should I eat it by myself? I can do it in a corner, on the kitchen floor, so I wouldn't disturb you!"

"Clover! Is that any way to treat a guest?"

"Mom, are you sure you want to be preaching to me at *this* moment?" She came over and placed her hand on Cade's shoulder.

"Clo, bring the dessert," Patrick said, trying to calm the situation.

"Right away – ladies and gentlemen!"

At that point Cade stood up, excused himself, and explained he had to make some important phone calls. Clover ran back. "Where are you going?"

"I left my cell phone at home…"

She followed him to the door. "Please, don't go…" she whispered.

"I just have to make a couple of calls."

Clover handed him her cell. "You can borrow mine…"

"No, I can't call from here," he gently smiled at her.

"Please, pleeease… shall I kneel? I beg you! *She* might hurt me, if you leave now…"

Cade chuckled, trying to interrupt her torrent of words, but Clover kept going.

"Tell me what you want. I will do *anything* you want, if you stay. I will help with all your Christmas gifts – no charge!"

He put his hand on the door knob. "I will come to bed with you!"

He turned, looking at her with a suggestive expression. Then he took her chin, lifting her face. "Sweetheart, I'm just going to make a few calls. I will be back."

"Why didn't you tell me this earlier?"

"I tried. You didn't give me a chance…" He laughed.

"Can you please hurry up?"

"I promise…" He stole a kiss from her – brief, but intense.

She watched him cross the street and forced herself to go back to the kitchen, leaving the door ajar.

As she returned, Nadia stood up. "You're really rude, Clover! How can you behave like that with a person like him?"

"Maybe I'm rude, Mom. But you are ridiculous. You were flirting with him!"

"How dare you?!"

"Listen Mom, you've monopolized the conversation all evening, you've ignored me every time I tried to say something…" Clover burst out. "What is bothering you? Is it that your poor, unattractive daughter has met a celebrity, while you haven't been able to, in spite of all your efforts? Are you afraid that Cade Harrison actually might be more interested in *me* than in *you*? Sorry to give you the bad news, but I think that's exactly what's happening this time!"

"Why? Are you sleeping with him?" Patrick asked with a serious tone.

"Not necessarily. It's because *she*'s old enough to be his mother! And because Cade is sick of people's flattery and adulation…"

"Sometimes I wonder whose daughter you are – where did you get this personality?" Her mother mumbled, irritably. "And now you've made him leave! Are you satisfied?"

"Cade just left for a few minutes. He will be back. So – put your swords away and pull yourselves together!" Clover put the cookie tray on the table.

"I wonder why a movie star like him should want to have dinner with us – ordinary mortals." Her brother was saying, with a perplexed tone. "Okay, so you helped him with his Christmas shopping, but it doesn't seem to me a good enough reason for him to join a small, boring family dinner party…"

"Well, evidently he finds me interesting enough to accept my dinner invitation – unlike your wife!"

Her last words silenced Patrick and the room became suddenly very quiet.

*

After about ten minutes and a few calls, Cade returned. He was happy with the idea that had occurred to him before he left her house.

Clover's birthday party had been a disaster. She hadn't had a good time at all, she had barely touched any food. Cade understood how she must have felt, although his own family was totally different – sometimes messy, but at least a very close family. They didn't fight for attention like that, nor were they so disrespectful of one another.

All evening he had been aware of Nadia O'Brian's sycophantic attitude towards him – not to mention her continuous flattery. Although he was used to adulation, at times he had felt frankly embarrassed. He had been kind and polite – it was his nature – plus they were Clover's relatives; yet it had been hard at times not to intervene to help Clover. He had tried more than once to bring the attention back to her –

after all she was the birthday girl! – but without success. Clover had pulled away from the general conversation, except for a few funny, sarcastic responses to her mother that had almost made him laugh out loud.

When he came into the house, he found the O'Brian family shrouded in an obstinate silence. Clover was standing near the refrigerator, with her arms folded across her chest. She seemed relieved to see him back and he flashed her an encouraging smile.

"My apologies to you all, but I couldn't postpone some important calls. I hope I didn't make you wait too long…"

"Not at all! Please, don't worry; it was just a pleasant break before the dessert…" Nadia O'Brian seemed to come back to life.

"Simple cookies," Clover said, sitting next to Cade. "It seems that birthday cakes have become obsolete. Did you know that?"

"Sweetie, you're not a child any more," her mother said. "Soon, you'll stop even celebrating birthdays…" and she giggled.

Cade put a hand on Clover's knee under the table in a comforting gesture. When he felt her small hand on his, he squeezed her fingers with affection. Neither of them could wait for the end of that dinner.

It lasted only another half an hour, but to them it felt like an eternity. When they finally moved into the living room, Patrick looked around and then asked if she had changed something. Clover looked at Cade anxiously, and he shook his head as if to say *no details…* so, she simply answered, "It was about time!"

At last it was time to open the gifts. Clover didn't expect any surprises. In fact, from her mother she received the perfume that she had specified on her wish list and her brother gave her a book. Probably this too, Cade thought, was something Clover had requested… yet he couldn't help but think that her brother could have done something more. The coldness of the whole scene shocked him. Maybe it was because he came from a family where everyone showed affection for each other. He felt the sudden urge to hug Clover and shower her with gifts, to somehow make up for her sadness and disappointment.

Finally, the O'Brians left. Cade sighed with relief and took Clover in his arms. She buried her face in his chest, whispering,

"It's finally over…"

"When you told me you had a difficult relationship with your family, I thought you were exaggerating… but Jesus! Anyway, my sweet Clover, now that the worst is over, what about going out – just the two of us?"

"Now? Seriously?"

"Isn't this what you usually do to forget your family get togethers? I'm not Zoe or Liberty, but I hope I could help you to…"

"I'm sure you can!" She flashed him a mysterious smile that suggested she might be entertaining other thoughts.

Her eyes were more luminous and suggestive than ever, maybe because of the joy of seeing the back of her relatives, or simply because of the wine. Looking at her, Cade felt his body waking up and a rush of desire went through him like a lightening. *Damn it! He had already organized everything, he couldn't change things at the last minute. Or could he?*

Clover put her hands on his chest, caressing him slowly. "It's already a wonderful diversion that you're still here, after the horrible evening I put you through!"

"That's a good reason to get out of here – you'll feel less guilty." Cade tried to focus on the present, trying to overcome the excitement and desire he felt at that moment. Maybe later they could return to *the subject.*

"Okay, take me out. Do I have to change or am I fine like this?"

Cade took hold of the edge of her t-shirt and took it off. There! Now you're perfect!"

"Such a rush! Confess – you too hate my poor t-shirt…"

"Right now I can't stand any of the clothes you're wearing." He laughed. "But I'll behave until later…"

"*Later?*"

"Am I mistaken or did you promise me something?"

"Oh – that was before you told me that you were coming back anyway!"

Cade grasped her hips, pulling her against him. "So, did you change your mind?"

"Umm… I'm not reasoning very well right now. No food and a lot of wine, plus the feeling of gratitude for having you as an ally tonight… all these things are definitely working in your favor! But it's unfair – since they might play against my better judgement."

"No worries! Since I want you sober, I won't take advantage of the situation." He took her hand. "Let's go."

When they stepped outside, the freezing air quickly cooled off any erotic fantasies they might have had.

"Where are we going?"

"To eat something… you need some food with all the wine you drank on an empty stomach!"

"And you? Will you watch me eat or do you still have some room?"

"There is always room for fat and fried food."

"Fat and fried?! Oh – that sounds great to me…"

9

The pizzeria near the Village seemed like a quiet place. Cade had made only one request, some privacy in spite of the fact that it was a restaurant.

"Pizza?" Clover smiled, looking at the illuminated sign.

"Well, I understood that formal dinners are not your style..." Cade joked, taking her hand.

"It's almost eleven. Maybe they are closing soon..."

"Don't worry." Cade opened the door for her.

"Surprise!" Zoe, Liberty and Eric shouted from a table at the end of the room.

The few people in the restaurant turned to look at them with curiosity. For a moment Cade regretted his idea. Perhaps he should have organized the party at his house. Anybody there could recognize him and spread the news. If the journalists found out, his peace would go up in smoke. But when he saw Clover's obvious delight at seeing the giant pizza and her friends, he thought that it was worth taking the risk. He wondered how many surprise parties had been organized for her before. Looking at her amazement and shining eyes, it was probably a sadly small number.

"Oh – my – god!" Clover said, coming over to the table. "This is definitely unexpected!"

Eric, Zoe and Liberty hugged and kissed her. Everyone had a little wrapped gift for her. Touched and confused, Clover thanked everybody. Then her eyes went to the huge pizza... "But the French fries spell out my name!" She looked at them bewildered.

Zoe nodded towards Cade, "His idea!"

Clover turned to look at him, speechless. He shrugged, saying, "I got this information from one of your tirades... I thought it was a great idea."

"You're *great*," she whispered, taking his face in her hands and passionately kissing him.

Cade felt immensely happy that it all turned out so well, and that the joy and surprise made her almost reckless. He hugged her and softly said in her ear, "Happy birthday, baby."

He realized that dining with them was a completely different experience from the evening with the O'Brian family. They were Clover's oldest friends and seemed to be in perfect harmony. They immediately included Cade in their conversation. They were friendly and funny, but most of all not one of them treated him like a celebrity. It was refreshing.

Throughout the evening, he began to get to know them a little. Zoe wasn't the *femme fatale* she appeared to be. She was an interesting young woman, who used this persona as a defensive shield to hide her emotional insecurities. On the contrary, Liberty's serious and inflexible attitude could be hiding a deep sensitivity that she may somehow fear. And Eric – with his nerdy spectacles – beyond his indisputable intelligence and great sense of irony, had a big heart.

After almost two hours of chatting, and lots of pizza and fries, they were all cheerful and also the only customers left in the restaurant. A young waitress kept bringing water or wine to the table, and every time she used the opportunity to look at Cade. She had recognized the movie star, but Cade was too relaxed to pay much attention to her.

They left very late. Clover said goodnight to her friends and Liberty told her she could take it easy and come in to the store later in the morning.

Walking to the car, Clover said, "Cade, I don't know why you did all this and I don't know how to thank you. I *only* know that I won't ever forget it!"

He came closer to kiss her, when he noticed a movement all too familiar to him. A man in a white car looked like he wanted to take a picture with his cell phone.

Shit! Cade got tense and sped up his pace. They got in the car. He got behind the wheel, but he kept checking the white car in the rear view mirror.

"Is there something wrong?" Clover was perplexed.

"I hope not…"

The guy in the white car was now taking pictures of some buildings. Maybe he was just a tourist after all and not a paparazzi. He shifted into reverse and turned into the street. Until now he had been able to hide his presence in New York, in spite of his wanderings with Clover. He began to really enjoy his holiday away from the media, and hoped that the journalists wouldn't spoil it.

After a few miles he noticed the white car in his rear view mirror. "Fuck!" he mumbled, pressing down hard on the accelerator.

"What's happening?"

"I think someone has recognized me and he's following us. It's the same car that was in the parking lot."

"God! I'm sorry…" Clover sighed.

Cade felt guilty. The evening might risk ending badly because of his famous movie star face. *Why don't they leave me alone? Fucking paparazzi!*

Upset, he abruptly made a U turn. "What are you doing?" Clover sat straight up.

"If that guy wants a scoop, I can make it easy for him… he can look me in the face!" he grunted angrily, now driving in the wrong direction, straight towards the other car!

Clover held onto the door. "Don't you think it would be simpler just to stop the car and talk to that guy?"

"If he's a journalist and I stop, tomorrow *everybody* will know where I am and who is with me… do you think it would be wise?"

"… no… of course not…"

Cade was staring at the white car. The street was almost deserted, so he wasn't taking a big risk. When he felt he had scared the other driver, he turned back into the proper lane. He almost had the impulse to open the window and flip him off, but thought the better of it.

Clover had a different idea. Quickly she opened her window, stuck her head out and shouted, "Too bad! Better luck next time! And Merry Christmas!"

Then she was quiet for a moment. She looked embarrassed. "I'm sorry. I couldn't help myself. I hope he didn't have time to take a picture of me…"

Cade shrugged. "A photo of somebody's head out of a car window – and not even my car – would get him nowhere. Also I'm not sure he was a paparazzi. He just had a cell phone, probably not a great photo quality anyway… also it's dark and it's snowing. Even if he did take a picture, you wouldn't be recognizable." He was talking mostly to himself.

But he suddenly thought, *of course, if that guy had been watching them since they arrived at the pizzeria, it would be a totally different story.*

"Well, if he got a picture of me, the worst case scenario is that we'll have a huge clientele tomorrow at the store!" Clover said, jokingly. Then laughing, she added, "My mother would die of envy, if she saw me tomorrow on the cover of one of her favorite tabloids! It would be almost worth hoping it—"

Cade felt suddenly uncomfortable at her words. When he had first met Clover, she seemed to be totally indifferent to publicity and gossip – actually, quite the opposite. Now she sounded much less worried than he was at the idea of being on the cover of a tabloid.

Was it possible that she was starting to enjoy it? Perhaps taking advantage of his celebrity didn't bother her after all. Maybe it was a way to get back at her mother, or get publicity for her store.

An inner voice spoke to him, while he observed her sweet profile. *What are you thinking? She's not like the others. She's probably simply playing down the episode to reassure you.*

He sighed. He didn't want to think about that and ruin this evening because of some paparazzi or because of his paranoia – clearly they were the result of his previous bad experiences with women. He wanted to continue to enjoy his vacation in New York, especially on this particular evening, and most of all with *this* woman.

He grabbed his phone and quickly dialled a number.

"Are you calling in reinforcements?" Clover asked.

"Hmm... yes, in a way..."

"Do you have you a policeman or a professional assassin at your service?"

Cade laughed. "No, but I have a good friend who is a pastry chef. He could help in another way. Didn't you say that chocolate is the best cure for any pain or trouble?"

She giggled, "But it's one o' clock in the morning! Your friend will be sleeping..."

A gruff voice answered the phone, "What the fuck do you want in the middle of the night?"

"Good to hear your voice, too, Zack! Did I disturb you?" Cade was laughing.

"What do you think?"

"You picked up after a few rings, so maybe I didn't disturb you enough. Listen, in a just a few minutes I will be near your bakery. Can you open it for me?"

"Give me a good reason for not telling you to go to hell," Zack yawned.

"Some paparazzi just nearly scared me and a friend to death. We need some chocolate to cheer us up, plus my friend here just turned twenty-eight and she hasn't had her well-deserved birthday cake yet."

He caught the sweet and warm look that Clover flashed at him and all his tension and worries vanished. *God – he would do anything for that smile!*

"Are you especially interested in this woman?" Zack was asking, as if he were reading his mind.

"Yes," he answered, locking eyes with Clover.

"Ok, I think I have something ready that could work. Send me a text with the girl's name and some information about her. But you must promise not to keep me up too long! You know how crazily busy we are during the holiday season…"

"I swear we'll be quick! Thanks, Zack."

As soon as he hung up, Clover giggled, "I'm impressed, Mr Movie Star! Your power must be incredible if you can get a pastry chef out of bed at this hour of the night! That guy must really be a good friend… or does he owe you money?"

Cade laughed again. "Actually, both! My fame helped him when he opened his bakery in New York, and I did loan him some money when he started out. I've known him for two years, and yes, I consider him a good friend."

Zack Sullivan was one of the few people he could definitely trust and that who hadn't approached him because of his public persona. Zack knew very well that if Cade wasn't having some serious and personal troubles, he would never have asked for his help.

"Still, you're a slave driver, Cade Harrison! Waking up a friend like this is inhumane…" Clover was amused and excited by the whole situation.

"But it was for an important cause! Any self-respecting birthday party must end with a birthday cake, and Zack is the best baker I know…"

"So, are you doing all this for *me*?"

"For you… and also for me. My forced *exile* has become a

fantastic vacation that I won't forget, thanks to you. So, you deserve a magnificent birthday cake!"

Clover didn't say anything.

Cade had wanted to tell her so much more, but he felt he had already exposed himself too much. It wouldn't be wise. Really. They hadn't known each other for long, and he was just recovering from one of the most stressful periods in his life. And he couldn't forget that his life was miles and miles away from New York.

He took the opportunity of a red light to send a text to Zack, then he turned near TriBeCa and headed towards the bakery. "Get ready to taste the most voluptuous dessert you can imagine!"

"I can't wait!"

Chocolate Sins Bakery was near Battery Park, not far from the port, with amazing views of the Hudson river and the Statue of Liberty. Cade parked in front of the store. Zack lived above it, so it shouldn't be too complicated for him to get downstairs.

Clover stared at the elegant sign, "Chocolate Sins!... It sounds good!"

"Zack is a real magician in the kitchen! I met him in San Francisco at a restaurant where he was the chef. But desserts have always been his passion, and a year ago he decided to open his own bakery here."

"I've never seen this place before, otherwise I would have remembered it... Oh – my – god! Look at this chocolate sculpture!" She was admiring a giant chocolate Christmas tree covered with a colorful sugar praline, standing in the window.

Cade knocked lightly on the glass and a few seconds later a tall young man with dark hair opened it.

"Hello, my friend! I know you hate me right now, but I am truly very happy to see you again..." he shook his hand.

Zack Sullivan hugged him. "Next time you come to New York give me a shout – maybe when the sun is up!"

"I promise..." Cade gently pushed Clover ahead. "This is Clover, the birthday girl. She has already had two birthday celebrations today – but not a single cake!"

"She can make up for that right here..."

"I'm sorry to barge in here in the middle of the night – but your VIP friend wouldn't listen!" Clover was very apologetic...

"No worries, lady. I was still awake... Come on in." He led

them towards the back of the store.

The sweetest of smells welcomed them, a mix of cane sugar, cinnamon, cocoa, marzipan and candied fruit… Clover was in total ecstasy! Cade noticed the way she inhaled deeply and looked around almost as if she were in a dream.

"Ok, leave me here forever, pleease!" she mumbled and Cade squeezed her hand, enjoying her contagious enthusiasm.

A huge cake, shaped like a Christmas star, was sitting on a table. Zack lit the twenty-eight little golden candles. Their glow illuminated the sugary surface where Clover's name was spelled out in chocolate.

"With my best wishes!" Zack handed them two champagne flutes.

Cade thanked him with a smile, but was looking at Clover's eyes, misty with tears. "Is this an optical illusion due to the candle light, or are you really crying?" he whispered in her ear.

She smiled warmly at Zack and her adorable dimples appeared, "Thank you, Zack!"

Cade felt a pang of jealousy. He knew this didn't make any sense – Zack deserved that smile and thanks, yet still he couldn't help feel… but he immediately relaxed when he felt Clover's slender arms around his waist. He was so happy that he forgot the paparazzi, his doubts about her reaction and their *unlikely* future together. What he really cared about right now was making her evening unique!

He embraced her tightly with his free arm and got lost in the sweet scent of her that was mingling with the bakery's even sweeter aromas. Only when he caught Zack's curious look, did he remember they weren't alone.

He kissed her on the cheek, "To Clover! Many happy returns!" They made a toast and Zack joined in.

After a sip of champagne, Clover walked round the cake, looking at it from every angle. "It's a masterpiece… it's a pity to eat it!" But in spite of her words, she extended a finger to get some of the chocolate crème and put it in her mouth. "Mmm…" Her little moan of pleasure excited Cade.

"Wait a minute – should I stay here watching her eat the cake, while you're eating her with your eyes?" Zack said under his breath to Cade.

"What?" Cade mumbled distractedly, while staring at Clover's tongue licking the cream from her full lips. He thought of tasting the cake directly from her mouth and hearing her moan – this time for a different kind of pleasure…"

"Man, you've really got it bad!"

At Zack's words, he could only manage a soft grunt in reply.

At that moment Clover grabbed her cell phone. "We need a photo now!"

"I'm afraid it's your turn, movie star…" Zack said to Cade in a low tone. He knew how these things worked… every woman eventually wanted a picture with Cade Harrison.

But Cade nodded, and whispered proudly, "She's different…"

Clover asked a surprised Zack to pose behind his amazing culinary creation, and took his picture. Then she picked up a spoon and threatened to shock everybody with the quantity of cake she would be able to eat…

"Wait!" Cade, amused, stopped her. "You must blow out the candles and make a wish."

"Right!" She bent over the cake and seemed to focus seriously on her wish. She smiled at Cade, who stared at her, mesmerized. The soft glow of the little flames created beautiful shadows on her elfin face. Her flamboyant red hair seemed alive and her big hazel eyes were glittering.

He felt a pulse of heat going through his body. Zack was right, he had really *got it bad*.

10

"I have a massive sugar high." Clover sighed, leaning back in the car seat. "Sugar must... have a strange effect on me, I can't stop giggling!"

Cade tried to focus on the road, it had snowed heavily. "You should have shown more self-control... I can't believe you had three huge slices of cake!"

"You can't bring a child to a candy store and expect any moderation! I've never had so much birthday cake in my whole life. I can still feel waves of pleasure and that sweet chocolate taste in my mouth..."

"You should feel light waves of nausea..." Cade laughed.

"The meringue looked like nimbus clouds... and the white chocolate... divine! I found everything a woman could want in that bakery: sublime ingredients, a fantastic smell and a gorgeous pastry chef who makes the best cakes in the world with unmatched elegance and sensuality..."

"Everything a woman could want! I'll tell Zack he has scored himself another victim!" he said, frowning.

Are you jealous? She thought, and the idea made her even more euphoric. "Well, he's a handsome man – it's difficult not to notice it. Tall, dark, mysterious... if I had met him on the street, I would think he was a fashion model. I would never imagine that a man like that was dealing with flour, eggs and ovens every day in the back of a bakery!"

"Ok, enough already... I get it!"

"Please, tell me he's not gay!"

"No, he's not..." Cade grumbled. "Listen, I'm driving and it's snowing, and if you keep provoking me like this, we'll have an accident!"

They had spent almost two hours in Zack's bakery. They all had a lot of fun. Zack let her taste several delicious cupcakes in addition to the cake! She thought it was incredible meeting another kind and fascinating man in just a few weeks. It was already a miracle to have met Cade!

After they left the bakery, Cade took her to see the river, such a sight under the snow! Now they were driving back to Staten Island, and she was thinking that no one before had done so many things to make her happy. It wasn't just the beautiful new sofa, the pizza party with her best friends and the birthday cake – there were many other details that had really touched her. She couldn't stop thinking of how he had helped her to get through the dinner with her mother, and his attentiveness throughout the entire evening. Everything he had chosen – down to the birthday cake – was something specifically thought of just *for her*. Her wish, when she had blown out the birthday candles, wasn't so different from her wish at the lighting of the Rockefeller Christmas tree. Maybe to express the same wish twice had strengthened her hope.

"I can't see anything with all this snow, but I think we've arrived."

Clover recognized the new Christmas lights now decorating her windows and, resigned, she gave a loud sigh. It was four o'clock in the morning and she was exhausted, but the idea of separating from Cade was unbearable. "Yes, we've arrived… my house is the only one still illuminated. I didn't expect to get home so late!"

"Do you regret it?" Cade pretended to be indifferent, but Clover wasn't fooled – not even for a second! She understood he was eager for her answer.

"You know perfectly well I'm not regretting anything! Do you need reassurance, Mr Celebrity?"

"Don't tease me, redhead!"

They got out of the car in front of Cade's garage. He was a few steps from her when his feet slipped on the ice and he lost his balance. He grabbed her arm and they both fell onto a big pile of snow on the side of the path.

"Are you ok?" he asked, trying to get back on his feet.

"Yes, and you?"

"Except for my deeply hurt pride, everything is fine…" he mumbled.

She burst into laughter, so contagious that he started to laugh too.

"You should have seen your face, so incredulous! You couldn't believe it, right?" she was laughing so hard, she cried.

"I *never* fall…" he looked at her, frowning, but his eyes were full of hilarity. "You're the one who's always got her ass on the ground!"

"The Prince of Hollywood went belly up in the snow! Justice has been served! I can't always be the clumsy one…"

"But I promise you, it won't happen again!"

"I wouldn't be so sure … Now that it's happened, you won't forget it, and then the fear of falling will make you clumsy and you'll eventually fall again… and I will laugh…"

A handful of snow hit her mouth, stopping her laughter instantly.

"That'll teach you! You can't tease a celebrity and hope to just get away with it."

Clover responded swiftly, throwing a big snowball at him. Then, while he tried to dry his face, she said, "It's not fair to take revenge on a poor, fragile woman who's sinking in the snow under the weight of a movie star."

"Oh – my god! Sorry! I'm crushing you. I didn't realize." Cade tried to get up, but she put her arms round his neck, happy to have him on top of her.

"You are not hurting me. The snow is soft…"

"And so are you," he smiled.

Hugging him, lying together on a big pile of snow, white snowflakes swirling around them, Clover thought that she had never been so happy before… ever. She looked at Cade's beautiful features and thought again about all the things he had done for her, and for the first time she felt really *unique*.

"It has been the best birthday of my whole life…" she mumbled, wanting to say much more.

He kissed her sweetly and passionately. She felt her body melting, in spite of the icy snow they were sitting in. That kiss seemed to last an eternity, yet she felt the longing for more when he let her go to stand up.

But then, embracing her tightly, he returned to her lips to kiss her more. She moaned, responding with all her desire. She realized only later that he was dragging her – still kissing her – towards his front door. He was able to unlock it – who knows how! – still keeping her tightly wrapped round him. Inside a pleasant warmth enveloped them.

Cade unbuttoned their coats and putting his arms round her waist, pulled her closer. Damn! All these winter clothes created such an irritating barrier! She caressed his chest, happy to hear his heart racing as fast as hers. She stood on tiptoe to reach his lips again, and he lifted her up. One of his hands slipped under her sweater and the contrast between his cold fingers and her warm skin, startled some clarity back into her mind, clouded by pleasure and passionate desire.

"My hands are so damn cold, I know," he whispered. "But they will get warm soon, I promise."

Clover nodded, but this sudden chill had re-activated her rational side. Yes, everything was magical. She just wanted to abandon herself in Cade's arms, lose herself in a vortex of passion, and spend the whole night – and beyond – in bed with him. Yet, she knew very well that Cade and this relationship were only an idyllic parenthesis in her life. Would she be able to return to her small monotone life after Cade's departure?

Her voice was trembling as she said, "I think I should go home now…"

"No way!" he answered, holding her even more tightly.

"I'm serious," she tried to move away. "This whole thing is a fantasy!"

"I don't agree," Cade took her face in his hands, searching for her eyes, "and you really don't agree either."

"Tomorrow we will regret this…"

"Not me, for sure!"

You are not risking your future peace of mind… she thought, looking down and stepping back. Yet, her hands were still holding his arms. She felt so ambivalent. It was so painful to really let him go. "We're too different, Cade."

"It doesn't look that way to me, not at this moment anyway."

"Tomorrow your mind will be clearer and you'll agree with me."

"I don't think so…"

Clover observed him. His face was tense, both because of his restrained desire and her sudden coolness. His hands, holding her waist, were warm now, and she felt his heat penetrate her skin and touch the nerves beneath it.

It would be easy – too easy – to surrender. She had never felt so tempted before in her life. Just the idea alone was powerful enough to scare her. To trust someone totally was unthinkable, without taking into account the fact that Cade was an actor –

someone who fakes emotions for a living. Yet, he seemed sincere right now and she wanted to take the risk so badly – maybe for the first time in her life. Although she knew how different their lifestyles were and that the probability of getting burned by this experience was high, a part of her still wanted to take the risk…

But, after a tough battle, the fear of being unable to deal with all these emotions prevailed over the desire to abandon herself. She did what she knew how to do best, get out of there!

When Cade saw her heading to the door, he rubbed his hands over his face, unable to stop her, and too discouraged to try. He let her go.

He wanted this woman, heart and soul. His desire went beyond the physical urge. Clover had somehow reached his heart. When she wasn't around, he missed her badly. It wasn't something he was used to feeling…

But he knew as well as she did that their relationship was a fantasy. She was right. They had very different lives and they lived far away from each other. Although he was rediscovering the importance of seizing the day and life's simple joys, he was acutely aware that his career, obligations and commitments waited for him in LA. It would be difficult at the very least to make everything compatible with Clover's life.

Yet, when he was with her, he forgot everything. He realized that her doubts were legitimate, but at this moment he just felt frustrated and angry. He took off his jacket, threw it on the floor and began to kick it… then he heard the doorbell. His heart jumped in his throat. It was four o'clock in the morning, the only person who could be behind that door was the person who left a few minutes before.

As soon as he opened the door, he saw Clover's face, reddened by the cold. She threw herself in his arms with a sigh. Cade hugged her and closed the door, his anger completely forgotten.

This time he wouldn't give her a chance to change her mind. He lifted her up and carried her into the bedroom, his mouth glued to hers. Once inside, he locked the door and – in front of Clover's confused gaze – put the key above the armoire. "You can't reach up there without my help," he said with a mischievous look.

"Basically this is a kidnapping!" she protested, but her eyes were burning with desire.

"Exactly." Cade took off her jacket.

"Kidnapping wouldn't be good for your reputation…"

"Well, I will just have to suffer the consequences!" Her sweater followed her jacket to the floor.

"Are you ready to blow your career for me?" She unbuttoned his shirt so hastily that the buttons almost popped off. "I appreciate your spirit of sacrifice."

"Good! Because I'm ready to martyr myself for the cause, until we collapse exhausted on this bed…" he began to pull off her pants. He felt her trembling as he ran his hands down the warm silky skin of her thighs. "Are you cold?"

"No, I'm just afraid of fainting in the middle of it…" she breathed heavily, coming closer to him.

Cade embraced her tightly. As soon as his body, stiffened by desire, felt hers surrender in its almost naked softness, his brain risked a blackout. "I've never made anyone faint before, but who knows… I could try, "he whispered in her ear, stroking her silky hair.

"If this is a challenge, I won't make things easy for you…" she began kissing his throat, moving her tongue slowly along the arch of his neck.

Cade felt a wave of heat and pleasure through his whole body. Clover realized it and whispered, "I've wanted to do this for a long time…"

"If we don't slow down, I'm afraid we'll both faint in a few minutes." He held her wrists, while her body was moving rhythmically against his.

"So then we'll have time to recover and continue our experiment *later*…" she smiled, allusively, and then kissed him with such urgency it left him breathless.

With a moan of defeat, Cade stopped thinking.

*

The relentless vibration of his cell phone woke him up. It was somewhere, maybe in his pants pocket – wherever his pants were! Still confused and groggy from lack of sleep, Cade tried to ignore the repetitive sound. He felt pleasantly relaxed after a fantastic night of passion with Clover, who was still sleeping at his side. He turned over to embrace her soft, warm body. He couldn't remember a more beautiful awakening. The house was warm and silent. Only a few muffled noises came from the snow covered street and a soft light filtered through the curtains. A wonderful woman, her legs intertwined with his and her radiant hair on the pillow, slept peacefully in his bed.

They had made love until dawn, collapsing, exhausted, only at the first light of day. If it weren't for that damn phone ringing, he would have slept much longer! Yet, being awake now, to observe the sweetest and most beautiful woman in the world sleeping so close to him was an incredible pleasure.

She had a relaxed expression and her sensual lips, even fuller and redder from the countless kisses, seemed to smile. Her wonderful red hair was spread on the pillow, exactly how he had imagined it so many times. He stroked her neck with his fingers, moving down along her shoulder, her back and her hips. Clover's sensitive skin reacted to his touch, and he revelled in it.

She belonged to him. Her milky skin still showed the marks of his passion and desire. Her sweet smell penetrated his fingers and his entire body. That amazing night had been not only an encounter of bodies, but something far deeper.

Suddenly, the thought of their future assaulted him. It was a continuous disturbing, gnawing thought. How to reconcile their lives, so different and so far away from each other? But he didn't want to give up yet. Not after he had gotten to know her.

He was tempted to wake her up to make love again, but he knew Clover had to work in the afternoon. She needed some sleep after that intense night…

The sound of the cell phone returned persistently. He decided to answer it, to check it wasn't anything serious. He finally found his pants and put them on, while checking the phone that had been in a pocket after all. He had received seven emails, eight voicemails, several missed calls, plus four texts – most of them from Scott. He immediately opened the texts.

> Let me know what to do. I don't know how you want to deal with the situation.
>
> They are driving me crazy. I'm under siege!
>
> Are you still sleeping? So, are the insinuations of the magazine correct…?

> Your press office is ready to broadcast any statement you want. But, please, don't make me wait too long! I may have a heart attack before the end of the day!

Cade cursed under breath and started to open the emails. He already imagined what they were about…

That bastard had actually done it! The guy in the white car had probably been called by someone in the pizzeria who had recognized Cade. He had lurked outside and taken several pictures through the windows with his cell phone. Damn it! Cade opened all the photos. Although the resolution was extremely low quality, his face and Clover's were perfectly recognizable. The pictures showed Clover and he as an intimate couple – although no shot showed anything explicit – and of course none of Clover's friends were in the pictures. In this way it really did look like a date. There was also a photo in which they were on the verge of kissing, before getting in the car. Scott had attached the article that appeared that morning in the *Enquirer*, together with the photographs. Cade read it with growing anger.

NEW LOVE ON THE HORIZON FOR THE PRINCE OF HOLLYWOOD?

No confirmation yet, but the pictures taken last night by one of our contributors speak for themselves.

The actor Cade Harrison, the subject this fall of a lot of gossip and speculation because of the hot, troubled ending of his relationship with the actress Alice Brown, is back in the news. Having disappeared from the scene for the last month, the handsome soldier of *No Man's Land* was caught last night with a mysterious red-haired woman, in one of New York's Greenwich Village restaurants. The couple had been seen in what appears to be an intimate situation, not taking their eyes off each other as they left the pizzeria together and got into a dark SUV.

Who is the woman who has won the attention of the most desired man of the moment? And how long has their relationship been going on? Cade Harrison seems to have recovered quickly from his break up with Alice Brown. Love at first sight for the redhead? Or just a romantic interlude in the magical holiday atmosphere of the Big Apple? We will keep you posted!

Cade left the bedroom, ignoring the other emails. While going down to the kitchen, he automatically dialled Scott's number. He wasn't sure yet how to deal with the whole situation.

"Jesus! Finally!" Scott answered at the first ring. "Where the

120

hell have you been?"

"Damn it! It's ten in the morning! Don't I have the right to sleep?" Cade burst out. "I just want you to shut those bastards up! I don't care how you do it. Just do it! I don't want any problems..."

"Unfortunately, homicide is not an option, so give me some other ideas on how to handle this."

"Make a statement in my name, but do not confirm *anything*. Fuck... at times I wonder, why do I have to go through all this shit?" He gave a loud sigh.

Cade had finally gained Clover's trust, and now his fame was threatening to ruin everything. He recalled how many times Clover had re-iterated that she didn't want anything to do with his world. But he was deeply immersed in that world, and he had absolutely no control over the gossip or the tabloids! Yet Clover had the right to choose and she should be protected from this mess. He really wanted to have more time to understand the nature of their relationship before facing the press. Something had begun between them, but it was too early to risk whatever it was because of some nosy publicity hound with a camera!

He had to stay calm; to stall as long as possible to repair any damage and to better understand what he and Clover had together. But he also needed to give the journalists a statement immediately to avoid them inventing a story about the mysterious red-haired woman.

"The fact is that we were with other friends at the restaurant! We were a group of five people... this is the point which you should insist on... and she's my personal shopper. I'm here to spend my Christmas holidays with my family and she helped me with gifts for them. I don't see anything wrong with that!"

"Yes, although usually dinner is not included with the shopping service..." Scott mumbled.

"Keep your comments to yourself! I want you to throw cold water on this story right away! I want this article to appear as a piece of trash, written by someone who didn't have anything more interesting to write about in his junk magazine! I did some shopping in New York and I was invited to a dinner party at a restaurant. That's all. I want to enjoy a vacation, as every young man of my age does – especially after that mess with Alice. Listen Scott, I definitely don't want them to upset this girl. They have to lose any and all interest in her. Immediately. Get it?"

"Well, to be honest, you two looked pretty intimate…"

"The quality of those shots is horrible… and I have pictures taken with my sisters, Heather and Cecile, that look more compromising than these… come on!"

"Okay, I will pass this information to the press office and let them deal with it. I will call you back to keep you posted."

Cade hung up. Then he listened to his voicemail messages. Some were from his mother and his sisters; they were curious to know about the news. He will have to give some explanation to them too. Fuck! It seemed that nothing in his life could remain unobserved and private…

Suddenly, he remembered that Clover was sleeping upstairs in his bed and wondered how he should tackle the issue with her. Maybe she would never even know about this article – she didn't read tabloids – if Scott could put an end to all this gossip right now. The idea of having to worry about his every step and every word, really bothered him. All this made him feel so sad, yet there was still some time before Clover had to go to work. He wanted to enjoy every minute of it. He decided to wait a while before telling her about the article.

When he returned upstairs, he found her awake, sitting on the bed. She wore his shirt which was way too big for her… she was still sleepy and so beautiful.

"Hey," he came over to her. "I thought you were still sleeping."

"I opened my eyes, and you had disappeared…"

"I went downstairs to get a glass of water." Cade sat next to her and hugged her. "Did you sleep well?"

"Well… but not enough." She buried her face in his neck.

"Why don't you call Liberty and ask her for a day off?" He caressed her back. "I promise to let you sleep for a few hours…"

"A *few* hours?" She looked at him with her eyes full of irony and expectation.

He felt a wave of desire and slipped his hands under her shirt, stroking her naked, hot skin. "Let's say a *few* minutes…"

Clover embraced him tightly. "This afternoon I have some important appointments, but I can stay until two o' clock. Why don't we go back to bed?"

"Don't you want some breakfast?"

122

"Food! With all that I ate last night? No thanks… I will be on a diet for at least a whole week!"

They went back under the blanket, the sheets were still warm. Embracing, they turned the TV on… Cade wouldn't have ever imagined that spending a morning in bed watching *Home Alone* could be so pleasant! But with her in his arms, everything was different: fun, exciting, sweet… Everything about Clover enchanted him. He felt at home with her.

Around one o'clock, after a quick lunch, Clover looked out of the window. "It's becoming really cloudy. If it starts raining, my afternoon will be very stressful…"

"I imagine it won't be fun going out shopping around the city in a storm." Cade was lying comfortably on the sofa.

"No, in fact… especially if your client is a mom who doesn't have a sitter for her little children, and has to bring them along to the appointment…" Clover sighed.

"Don't go! Stay with me."

"I would love it…" Clover seemed undecided and came over to him.

Seeing her sitting on the sofa's arm, Cade thought maybe he had convinced her. He put his arm round her shoulders, trying to pull her closer. "Did you change your mind and will you stay with me?"

She leaned over him, whispering, "It sounds very promising, but… actually, I was just looking for this!" smiling, she showed him the remote control in her hand.

Cade sighed with disappointment. "I'm here, completely at your disposal, and you want to watch TV!"

Clover laughed, "I just want to check the weather report!"

While she was searching for the channel, Cade pulled her over to sit on the couch next to him. "If they say it is going to pour with rain all afternoon, will you stay at home?" He kissed her neck.

"No, but I could cancel a couple of the later appointments."

"Okay, I will try to be content with that." Cade bent over to kiss her, when he heard his name mentioned on CBS news. He felt paralyzed. He should have known: news spreads quickly.

The journalist was briefly reporting the scoop about Harrison's new love interest. Cade, worried about Clover's reaction, focused more on her face than on the screen. He saw her eyes widening, while the images of the photos were shown.

At first she looked incredulous. Then she became serious, as she concentrated on the news, but her expression was inscrutable.

After the news, there was the weather forecast, but neither of them paid much attention to it.

"I'm sorry," he mumbled, examining her face for reaction.

"It's ok… I'm not too bad in those pictures," she surprised him with a cheerful smile.

"Don't you care about appearing in a trashy tabloid? Doesn't it bother you that everybody will speculate about us?!" Cade asked, deeply confused by her reaction. "Are you aware that they will come looking for you! Right now, they will be trying to discover who you are…"

"What can I do about it? I can't go around wearing a ski mask for the rest of my life!" Clover stood up, "Don't worry about it. The reservations at the pizzeria weren't in our names, and the car is not yours. It would take a while before they discover my identity and the place where you live now…"

It will take much less time than you believe… Cade thought, discouraged. The media worked better than the FBI, when celebrities were involved!

Clover gave him a light kiss on his lips. "I'm going home to change and then I'll run to the store. Will I see you tonight?"

"Sure…" Cade watched her as she put on her jacket and left the room – not the least bit upset, but with a calm, peaceful expression and bright eyes. He wondered why he had thought that the situation would shake her confidence… he had imagined her creating a scene, a big drama, protesting against the invasion of her privacy. On the contrary, she seemed almost… prepared for the possibility of this event.

Once again he felt a pang of uneasiness. He didn't want to believe the remote possibility that Clover *had hoped* that something like this could happen. No, it wasn't possible! Yet, some doubts kept gnawing at him… he couldn't honestly deny that Clover's attitude towards his celebrity life had changed dramatically since their first few encounters. What had caused her change of heart?

11

"Here she is, our star!" Zoe exclaimed, as soon as Clover stepped into the store.

"What are you talking about?" she asked, but she had an amused smile on her face.

"Look at you! You have the classic expression of someone who spent the entire night rolling around naked in bed with the sexiest man alive!" Zoe shook her head, pretending to hold a grudge. "Now I'm the one who envies you!"

"Stop! It's not what you think…" Clover tried to protest, but soon she burst into laughter, saying, "Actually, it's exactly what happened!" She collapsed on a chair and covered her face with her hands… she was blushing just at the memory of her night with Cade. "I'm still floating in a river of ecstasy… I can't believe it's true!"

"It's not an everyday thing to be the chosen one of a Hollywood star!" Zoe sat next to Clover at her desk. "So – how was it? Is he good in bed? Is *everything* as beautiful as it looks?"

At that moment Eric came in the room. "Let me guess, Zoe! Are you asking for details about Cade Harrison's sexual attributes?"

"Clover is the best source for this… this kind of information is not available in tabloids." Zoe focused again on Clover, who was smiling mysteriously.

"I would never tell you any details like that!"

"You're cruel and ungrateful!" Zoe shrugged, "however, looking at your insanely happy expression, I already have my answer…"

Clover didn't reply – her dreamy smile still on her face.

"And what about the rest? Is everything fantastic?"

"Much more than fantastic… It's like a dream. Seriously, almost too good to be true."

"Try not to bring bad luck to yourself!"

"You know, I don't believe in those kinds of things," she

looked at her friend with shining eyes. "Zoe, I don't know if this *thing* will last, or even how we could carry it off, especially now that the media have found out that Cade is in New York. But I know that nothing like this has happened to me in my entire life! I feel dangerously close to desperately falling in love with him – so, help me god!"

"Have you talked about what's happening between you two?"

"No... everything has happened too fast. I'm not sure what Cade is thinking. I know he is attracted to me," she thought of the last hours with him, she recalled his passion and blushed again. "*Very* attracted to me. Beyond that, I don't know anything else..."

"For sure it's not only about sex. I've spoken with him on the phone, when he contacted me to organize the surprise party at the pizzeria. It was clear to me that his desire to surprise you was genuine. He had noticed how sad the dinner with your mother and brother was, and he wanted to do something to cheer you up. He has been very sweet."

"Yes, this is what I adore about him." Clover stood up and started to walk around the room with a dreamy expression. "He's so sensitive and generous. He listens to me and cares about what I want. He makes my heart race, like nobody else does..."

"I'm sure that everything will go well, in spite of those obnoxious journalists." Zoe encouraged her.

Clover huffed, bothered just by the thought of the episode. "Cade has immediately become very nervous about that article. The journalists that invade his privacy really drive him crazy – especially after all the mess he went through with his ex..."

"And you? How do you feel about being at the center of all this latest gossip?"

"I hate it! And I'm also terrified... It bothers me a lot, but I've restrained myself with Cade. I pretended to be almost indifferent when we watched the news together. I don't want Cade to worry about me, but I hope the media will take a while before they find out who I am..."

"On the contrary, it will take very little time!" Liberty said, entering the office and putting a copy of the *Enquirer* on the desk. "I have already received several calls from our clients asking if *you* are really Cade Harrison's new girlfriend. I've pretended that I didn't know anything about it. However, clearly many of them have recognized you. The word will get around at the speed of light!"

Clover came over to the desk with her heart in her throat and looked at the magazine. She felt a strange sensation seeing herself with Cade on these pages that showed a few moments of the most magical evening of her life. It was the first time for her – a simple and anonymous girl – to hit the headlines... *how does it feel to make news? Frankly, like hell!* She already felt very stressed and she could only imagine how Cade must have felt all these years.

"Anyway, they don't have anything. These pictures only show two people eating in a pizzeria!" Clover burst out.

"And there were *five* people! They could at least put all of us on the cover... that would be fun," Zoe said, to lighten the atmosphere.

But Clover was seriously starting to worry. This whole article spoiled her joy. It was especially the uncertainty of not knowing what Cade thought that made her anxious.

"How should we deal with the situation here at the store?" Eric asked, pragmatic as usual.

"If this story continues, it will be hard to contain the client's curiosity, and the publicity could be good for the store... However, I absolutely don't want to fuel any gossip," she was specifically addressing Zoe and Eric, who spent most of their time at the store. Then she turned to Clover, "You do your best to protect yourself from the paparazzi. We'll decide how to deal with the situation later, depending on how it all evolves."

Clover nodded. She knew that sooner or later something like this would happen. If her relationship with Cade had a future, she needed to get used to it. This was the main reason that had stopped her from making a drama about the gossip. Now that she knew her own deep feelings, she should be flexible towards Cade's career, accepting it's down side.

It would be impossible to keep their secret forever. She didn't want her privacy to be invaded by the media or by curious people, yet she didn't want to be forced into hiding either. Cade cared about her. She was sure of this. Therefore, even though it was too early to make plans about a future together, she felt they would be able to withstand the gossip in one piece.

She left the room to start working, but she couldn't help hearing Zoe say, "They are so sweet together! Did you notice how he looked at her last night?" Clover stopped just behind the door.

"We should take it easy on guessing…" Eric said. "They have just met and we don't know how Harrison feels. He was in New York to hide from the paparazzi; now that they have found him, he may decide to fly back to LA as soon as possible."

"I can't believe that Clover doesn't mean a lot to him. He organized a surprise party for her birthday and was been so sweet and caring with her all evening. That must mean something!"

"Yes, that he wanted to take her to bed! And he succeeded, actually…" Eric said, cynically. "A man like that doesn't have to make too much effort to get what he wants."

"Jesus, Eric! Did you wake up in a bad mood this morning?" Zoe burst out.

"No, I'm just trying not to fall into female sentimentality, like you do. We don't know this guy; we can't be sure he's in love with Clover after just one week."

Zoe continued stubbornly, "I'm sure he's not acting… trust me. I know immediately when a man is in love with a woman. I have a nose for this kind of thing…"

"Sure you do!"

Liberty interrupted their conversation, "Okay, now get to work, guys! We'll discover what the truth is very soon. In case you happen to be right, Eric, let's be ready to help our little Clover. She seems to really be in love with Cade Harrison. I hope that she won't regret her trust in him."

Clover left the store in silence, her mind invaded by thoughts. Cade was a celebrity, so it was absolutely normal that the journalists had an interest in him and in the people around him. Especially after his tumultuous breakup with his ex, the media, of course, were curious, seeing him with a new, unknown woman. Yes, it was all understandable, so – why did she feel so anxious? She had a bad feeling.

She and Cade hadn't discussed their feelings yet. Nor had they talked about a lasting relationship between them. She had tried to resist this powerful attraction, exactly because she feared an uncertain future. Now, making love to him had only strengthened her feelings and it would be harder than ever to be without him – to start over. But was it necessary? Cade liked her and she liked him – actually, she *definitely* liked him!

This gossip had come at the wrong time, too early. She would have preferred to discuss the situation with him before appearing on a tabloid cover. Yet, why shouldn't their relationship eventually work? She just hoped that obnoxious, curious people could leave them alone.

But luck wasn't on her side. All the clients she met on the street assaulted her with questions about Cade. Not even the pouring rain could stop them! She was walking fast, but with the persistent feeling that everyone looked at her with curiosity – as if she had appeared on *The New York Times* front page as President Obama's secret mistress!

She found this sudden interest in her intrusive and absurd. She decided to tell her clients that she had simply helped Cade Harrison with his family's Christmas shopping. She tried to say as little as possible. Firstly, she wanted to discuss the best strategy with Cade.

She was returning home when she heard her cell phone ringing. She hoped it was him. She hadn't heard from him all afternoon, and her mistrustful side had begun to imagine the worst. Was he angry because of the article? She remembered his anxiety and even paranoia about being recognized during his first days in Staten Island. And the night before, when he understood that the white car was following them, he looked really furious... or had he already had enough of her? Just the thought made her shiver.

Hearing his voice was a joy and relief, although his tone wasn't enthusiastic at all. He sounded tired, nervous... maybe bored?

"I got your cell number from Zoe... hope you don't mind."

"Of course not..."

"Is everything okay? Have people recognized you on the street? Did they ask you strange questions?"

He got right to the point, Clover thought. She sighed, "Nobody offered me any money for an interview, if this is what you are thinking. I had to answer questions to a couple of curious clients, but I didn't say anything compromising. I just said I helped you with Christmas shopping."

"Perfect!" he sounded relieved and Clover felt a pang of disappointment.

"Has anyone followed you?"

"Jesus, Cade! Am I ending up in some trashy spy movie?" she mumbled, a little too sharply. She was in a taxi and she turned to check behind... "I see two cars behind me. The people driving could have a camera, some binoculars, a pad and a pen... which weapon should I fear most?"

"Clover, it's not funny. If the journalists find out where I live, it will be the end of my peaceful vacation."

"Like it is my fault! I didn't choose to go to that pizzeria – just to refresh your memory – and it's not me that the paparazzi follow. *I* should be the one that is upset by this whole story, and you should be accustomed to this mess! But, on the contrary, you seem to be freaking out – like on the verge of a nervous breakdown..."

"Wait a minute, your calmness sounds strange to me, since you always seemed to deeply despise everything to do with my life and profession..."

Clover felt a knot in her throat, "What do you mean? Would you prefer to see me pulling my hair out and howling?"

"I would prefer not hearing you sound almost satisfied..."

"I'm *not* satisfied! Last night everything was beautiful, and I would definitely prefer to remember it without the pictures in a trashy tabloid. But it has happened and we can't do anything about it... actually it could happen again."

Cade sighed, "You're right. Sorry, I'm very stressed. I just don't want them bothering us."

"I'm almost at home." Clover held her breath, hoping that he would ask her to join him right away. But Cade remained silent and her heart sank. "Perhaps it might be better if we don't see each other tonight, don't you agree?"

"If someone has followed you, they will control what you do and where you go. If you come over here, they will wonder why..."

He doesn't want to see me... she thought. It had only been four hours since she hadn't seen him, and she already missed him so much.

"I understand... I don't want my neighborhood to become a reporters' camp site either, especially as I will have to live here much longer than you." Clover closed her eyes and took a deep breath. "Don't worry, I won't even glance at your house." She got out of the taxi and went straight to her door, without looking back. "Here! I am inside. I locked the door and I promise I won't open it to strangers. You can relax now..."

"Relaxing will be difficult," Cade sounded really worried. "I had hoped to have more time to enjoy New York, but they have found me. And now that they have seen you too, things are going to get a lot more complicated."

"How long do you think all this will last?"

"It depends..." Cade hesitated and Clover sat on the couch, legs shaking.

"It depends on what?" she asked cautiously.

"It depends on us."

Is there an 'us' with us? She wondered. At that moment she heard the beep of a call waiting. "Someone is trying to call me." She felt almost relieved to interrupt that embarrassing silence.

"I had hoped for a different kind of evening, Clover. I'm very sorry... now that we have started..."

...now that we have started to have fun... she thought bitterly. But then she remembered Cade's sweetness and felt guilty. "Yes, I feel the same way. Let me know how you want me to deal with the situation in the next few days. Good night, Cade."

She hung up and took the waiting call. It was her mother...

"Clover, I must confess that reading the *Enquirer*'s article took my breath away. At your birthday dinner I believed Cade when he said that you were simply his personal shopper. But then both your brother's insinuations and this article made me think that you have hit the target this time!"

"Come on, Mom, get to the point..."

"It would have been a big score for you, Clover! A *great* score, actually... too bad there is nothing going on between you and Cade Harrison."

Clover felt a chill down her spine, "How did you arrive at this idea? If I'm not wrong, the article suggests the opposite..."

"Yes, the article... but Cade's denial has been quick and, and in my opinion, almost excessive. After all he should be used to rumors about his many fictitious flirtations... he could have waited a little bit and let you enjoy a few days of fame!"

"I don't know what you're talking about, Mom."

"Really? Cade Harrison's official statement appeared online a few hours ago. Look for it and read it, you're mentioned too." Then her mother's voice sounded sad. "I'm sorry sweetie, maybe this time you've aimed too high. He's a very famous actor, incredibly successful. A man like him can have everything he wants from life. It's impossible to believe that someone like him could fall for a normal woman."

Clover ended up the call. Her heart felt as if it was going to jump out of her chest. She hadn't even digested the *Enquirer*'s article yet and now more news… An official denial by Cade?

She rushed to the computer and typed Cade's name. She was overwhelmed by news and links about him, but after narrowing her search to the last couple of days, she found the news she was looking for.

NO NEW LOVE ON THE HORIZON FOR CADE HARRISON. "SHE IS JUST MY PERSONAL SHOPPER."

The stolen photographs – that appeared in this morning's Enquirer showing the actor Cade Harrison with a mysterious redhead have created quite a stir that has generated a lot of attention and rumors. But the whole story seems to be just a soap bubble. In fact, a few hours ago we received the official statement from the hero of No Man's Land, who denies any new love relationship.

Harrison, who is in New York for a vacation to recover after the stress of his tumultuous breakup with the actress Alice Brown, declared that he is very upset by the tabloid's article. He has clarified that the young woman, who appears with him in those pictures, is simply his personal shopper.

"I don't have anything further to say about this story. I am spending some free time shopping for Christmas gifts and I had simply accepted a birthday party invitation. I try to have a good time during my holidays, like every other normal young man has the right to do… I think I deserve it, especially in the light of a very stressful period in LA. The shots that show me with that young lady have been artfully chosen to create a scoop – they don't demonstrate anything. I have more compromising photos in my family album than these! I attended a dinner in a crowed pizzeria with a small group of normal young people, something that rarely I have a chance to do, because of my profession. Frankly, I don't understand all this interest in seeing me just chatting with a woman whom I barely know. Since I've become famous, the media has attributed to me innumerable relationships and affairs. Honestly, there's no way that I could even have the time for all these women!"

So, no new love for the Prince of Hollywood. We wonder if he is still suffering for the beautiful Alice Brown. Is this statement intended to reassure his ex? The actress doesn't seem to have forgotten him yet. Last week she appeared at a charity event in LA, looking seriously skinny and very pale.

Clover's head suddenly felt heavy and her throat was on fire. She stopped reading, her vision blurred. Cade's words were echoing in her mind… *I am trying to have a good time during my holidays, like every other normal young man has the right to do… The shots that show me with that young lady have been artfully chosen to create a scoop – they don't demonstrate anything. I have more compromising photos in my family album than these…*

… A good time? Had she only been this for him? A fleeting moment of fun – like a bachelor party – after his breakup with the beautiful Alice, who was perhaps still waiting for him in LA? She felt overwhelmed by a wave of disturbing thoughts. She recalled her mother's words and those of Eric… and her own conscious and unconscious doubts resurfaced.

Cade was a celebrity, gorgeous and very rich: he was definitely out of her league. His attention and sweetness, his kisses and passionate caresses, had made her forget he was an actor, and in fact a very skilled actor! He had convinced the whole country to view him as a dying soldier… so to convince a silly young woman like her that he was in love should be a piece of cake!

Tears of disappointment, pain, and anger streamed down her face. Now she understood why he hadn't called her all afternoon. He knew that he had released that hateful statement and didn't know how to tell her. He probably hoped to have a little more time for *fun*, but he had been caught in the act and now had to change his plans quickly. His public image was at stake, maybe he even had problems with his ex… He hadn't worried at all about her feelings when reading that statement… his only concern was to make sure the paparazzi wouldn't discover where he lived.

Feeling physically ill, she suddenly stood up and went over the window to check the street. Cade's suspicions were right: someone had followed her. A man was sitting outside on a low wall, and for sure he wasn't there just to get some fresh air in the snow!

"Damn it!" She threw her hat on the floor. Well, if Cade didn't give a shit about her feelings, neither did she about his. She wouldn't remain silent and simply endure this humiliation. She flew out of the house, furious, and knocked on Cade's door with all her might. She looked back and noticed that the reporter was now standing, pretending to be indifferent…

Cade opened the door, but remained in the shadows.

"Clover! Damn it! A guy has followed you, didn't you notice him?"

"Yes, I've noticed him, but I don't care, you *butt signing* asshole!"

Cade took her hand, quickly pulling her inside, and closed the door. She thought that this move would confirm the reporter's suspicions.

"What's going on?" Cade asked her, still checking the journalist's movements in the street.

"I have just a couple of things to say to you... and, unlike you, I want to say it to your face!"

"What?"

"Don't pretend you don't know! I read your denial online, and what really bothers me is that it was *my mother* who told me about it... and I, being so naïve, thought *you* might have told me!"

"Tell you what?"

"...that I have been nothing but a quick little fling for you! A bit of fun! A rebound to recover after your stressful breakup with your ex, a worthless Christmas afterthought!" Clover felt a lump in her throat, but she didn't allow herself to cry. She didn't want to give him that satisfaction too.

Cade seemed sincerely confused, but now that she knew his actor's talent so well – he couldn't fool her any more. "Is this one of those moments when you get totally carried away, and there's no chance of stopping you?" he asked, trying to win her over with a smile.

"Don't dare use your charm with me!" Clover continued, getting more furious and shaking her finger at him. "After your official statement, you don't need to make any useless effort... it's too late, now that you went public!"

"What's the matter, Clover? Are you angry because of my denial? What did you want? Would you really want me to confirm everything?" Cade looked more and more perplexed.

"Confirming *what*... That you're seeing a *stranger*? Oh no! Your ex is still waiting for you, skinny and pale; so you can't spoil everything by saying that you're dating another woman!"

"Listen, Alice has nothing to do with us, and you know it very well."

"I know just one thing very well: you did a lot for me for the pure purpose of getting me into bed! You didn't have to work too hard, right? Who knows? Maybe this whole story may be good for me too, eventually. To fuck a movie star… it doesn't happen so often, right?" Clover smiled, resentfully. "I will tell this story for years to come… and if people don't believe me, I can always show them the sleazy tabloid pictures – in fact, why don't I just frame them for future generations!"

Cade's hurt and sad gaze seemed authentic. "Seriously, is *this* all you're getting at?"

Clover was puzzled. He didn't understand anything. To take the time to wonder about his reaction could have changed her mind, but instead she was feeling even more embittered and disappointed. "You wanted to act the role of Prince Charming and I let you do it. It's evident now that even on holiday you need to be an actor… you need people to remind you who you are! You told me this, and I didn't forget it." She squeezed her fist until she felt her finger nails sticking painfully into her palms. "You could have spared yourself all that mushy, corny stuff! You could have gotten straight to the point. Just a good fuck and we wouldn't even end up on a tabloid's cover. Too late." She gave him an icy look and moved towards the door. Her rage was leaving her, making way for a growing sense of sadness and a strong desire to cry. She needed to leave that house, immediately.

"I can't believe what you just said." Cade said with husky voice.

Clover stared at him. He looked hurt, angry, sad, and incredulous, but she was too upset and confused to understand whether or not he was being sincere. She shrugged. "It's not important. Also I don't believe anything a consummate actor says."

"You couldn't be more wrong, Clover."

Clover gave him a half smile. "Let's be serious, Cade. Even if it were all true, it wouldn't last anyway."

"How can you know that?"

"Listen, you and I are worlds apart, literally. Why would you want a *young lady* who is normal anyway? My mother is right, you're out of my league! For a moment she was afraid that she would have to congratulate me, but after your *very* public denial, she breathed a sigh of relief."

"What the hell should I have done?" Cade moved towards her. "I suppose I could have confirmed everything… and then what?"

"Oh – do you mean after your return to LA? Well, I would be written off as Cade Harrison's Christmas' love affair – I guess that's still better than being described as less compromising than a family photograph!"

"If it's so important to you, I can still give you some notoriety. It would be enough if I were to kiss when you leave, in front of that reporter outside. But do you know what will be written on the papers tomorrow? That I was giving a farewell kiss to my secret mistress before returning home. Yes, because now going back to LA is the only rational thing I can do, since you showed that journalist where I live!" He passed a hand through his hair, his eyes suddenly expressionless. "Sorry if I didn't give you more coverage in the tabloids. I'm so stupid to think that I was doing you a favor!"

"You're doing me a favor now." Clover backed towards the door, "I don't give a damn about missing the chance to bask in your bright reflection!"

She ran home, her sight blurry. Yes, he should go back to LA! It was the best solution, so she wouldn't be forced to see him around. It should serve as a lesson for her! Just in case she might be so stupid another time, deluding herself about the possibility of living a fairy tale.

Cade believed that she was looking for fame, anxious to let the whole world know she made love to a movie star – he obviously had a very low opinion of her!

She began sobbing as soon as she got back home. The Christmas paraphernalia inside made her feel even worse. The lights, the decorations, the mistletoe, all seemed to mock her and emphasize her sense of loneliness and failure. She had made that stupid wish during the lighting of the Rockefeller Christmas tree under the illusion that it would be heard – such a silly girl!

To tell the truth, even though she actually *had been desired* by a man like him – this wasn't what she really wanted. The wish she was granted lasted for only a fleeting moment – it wasn't going to last for life.

Her fleeting moment with Cade Harrison had already gone.

12

He had forgotten how hot the blazing sun could be in California, even in December. It was strange to wear just a t-shirt instead of a heavy sweater... strange to hear the sound of ocean waves instead of the muffled silence of the snow. It felt odd to be in the huge villa, that he once considered his refuge and which now seemed so empty.

The Christmas songs on the radio seemed out of place in a city without snow and a holiday atmosphere. This music sounded wrong in a place without Clover. He hadn't seen her for two weeks, and he missed her as if he hadn't seen her for years! He kept thinking of the few intense days they spent together, full of passion, sweetness and cheerfulness. He was touching the snow globe that she gave him, repeating to himself how foolish he had been.

He had been unable to deal with the whole situation. When he gave the statement to his press office, he didn't realize how cold and impersonal it might sound. Actually, he was used to ignoring gossip and rumors, both true and false. In this case, with his denial, he wanted to protect Clover, and the intimacy that was beginning to grow between them. Instead, the result had been a disaster.

He had left New York that same evening, with bruised feelings and heartache at the thought of never seeing her again. Instead, he saw her on TV only two days later! Apparently, the paparazzi had been lurking outside her house, trying to figure out how she was dealing with his sudden departure for LA. They didn't get very far. The brief video clip showed only a young woman, walking alone, apparently quite calm, her face partially hidden by a scarf. But for him to see her like this had been like an awful punch to the gut. His sweet, bubbly Clover seemed like a ghost in those images. She walked with her head down, dressed all in black. The only note of color was her red hair peeking out from under her hat. Cade would give anything to see her smile with those adorable dimples again... even more to know what she must be thinking.

The doubt that she had just been using him for publicity and ambition had tormented him for a while. But deep down he knew that Clover, behind her mischievous elf mask, was incredibly honest and not a social climber at all.

Let's be serious, Cade. Even if it were all true, it wouldn't last anyway... Listen, you and I are worlds apart, literally. Her words were haunting him, and he couldn't stand the thought that she might have considered him to be a liar the whole time.

Was Clover truly convinced that a future for them together wasn't possible? Hadn't she really understood how important she had become for him in such a short time?

He didn't know how to show her that he was crazy about her. He wanted her to believe that he didn't *act*, although he was an actor... he had thought hundreds of times to write, or to call her. He had even thought of mailing her the check for her work as his personal shopper, a thing that probably would make her angry. Given her explosive temper, she would probably take a flight to LA just to give him a piece of her mind – right to his face! Actually, it would be wonderful to open the door and find her right there...

At that moment he heard the doorbell and almost laughed. *Something like this doesn't happen even in a B movie*, he thought, opening the door. Yet, his heart was beating fast and he felt a deep disappointment when he saw his mother. His face must have betrayed his feelings, since Grace Harrison said with an ironic tone, "You seem disappointed, sweetie. Were you waiting for someone else?"

"Mom, did you come to lecture me?" Cade sighed, letting her in.

"I did!" she exclaimed, smoothing her long blonde hair with her hand. "Your brother told me you're not sure if you want to come to New York with us. Is this true?"

"His status of favorite son has sure made Jake a real big mouth..." Cade mumbled, perching on the arm of the sofa.

"... and this really helps a mother who has become too old to deal with her children's tantrums a lot." Grace shook her head with a tired air, "Cade, I didn't think you were such a coward. I find your behavior truly disappointing."

"What are you talking about?"

"First you run away from LA to avoid a confrontation with Alice, instead of facing her and telling her directly everything she deserved to hear, especially after all her lies and the mess she created for you with the media. You decide to hide in New York and force whole your family to go there for Christmas, so you wouldn't be alone. Then you fall for a girl, the paparazzi catch you in the act, and what do you do? You run away again and return home with your tail between your legs!"

"As far as Alice is concerned, you know very well that I simply didn't want to sink to her level. Actually, I even said too much. She didn't deserve an ounce of my consideration!"

"I'm afraid that I am in partly guilty for that story. I've trained you too well… and anyway, that bitchy woman, catting around like that, deserved much worse…" his mother huffed, making him smile, "but what about the other girl?"

"Clover," Cade enjoyed pronouncing her name.

"Yes, Clover," His mother repeated with a smile. "She has impressed you like no other girl has ever before. You were in New York for only three weeks and you've come back with goo-goo eyes!" Cade's surprised glance didn't escape Grace. "Do you think I'm so naïve? Every time we spoke on the phone, you took every chance to say her name, before and after the *Enquirer*'s article. Also, you had such a furious reaction to that article, it made me immediately suspicious. But this time too, instead of showing your real feelings, you just retreated into your safe *little shell.*" She stared at him with blue eyes so similar to his. "I wonder why you are hanging out here, if you like her so much…"

Cade rubbed his tired face. "She doesn't trust me, Mom. She thinks that my success complicates things between us and makes us too different. And perhaps she isn't so wrong…"

His mother came over to him. "Cade, if you had told the whole world what you truly felt for her, do you think Clover would still be concerned about your fame?"

"Honestly, Mom, I'm not sure about what she feels. It wouldn't be the first time that a woman is just interested in what I represent," he looked up at the only woman he had ever trusted completely, finally dropping his defensive shield. "Last time we talked, she said some things… things that made me think that our encounter was for her only a game, a challenge, a dream… yet, I didn't believe her completely. I never had the impression that she was a woman hunting for fame. My instinct tells me she was trying not to show she was hurt by my public denial. I saw her acting the same way with her family, when she felt hurt…"

"So, what is holding you back?"

"I don't know… I'm still doubtful. I know her so little. I think she has an extreme need for certainty and attention… maybe she really wanted the exposure on that tabloid cover to feel special."

Grace rolled her eyes at the obtuseness of her very beautiful son. "You inherited a big flaw from your father, sweetie: the inability to understand women, if someone doesn't explain to you exactly how to deal with them!"

Looking at her proud frown and listening to her lecture, Cade smiled, "In fact now I am beginning to understand Dad and feel real sympathy for him!"

"Listen, darling, if Clover needed that kind of media exposure to feel special, you have been lacking in many respects." Grace almost laughed, seeing her son's puzzled expression. "However, if, on the contrary, she's a proud girl who attacks so she can hide her need for love from the world, well, you certainly demonstrated a real lack of sensitivity when you denied everything to the press office."

"So, it's my fault either way?"

"I'm afraid I have to say yes."

Cade gave a heavy, resigned sigh. "So, what should I do?"

"Can't you figure it out?" She huffed with a sense of exasperation. "You should go and get her back!"

"And if I am wrong? If she is not the person I think she is… if she didn't truly feel what I feel…"

"You will suffer, son, but at least you will know that you've tried…" his mother looked at him with tenderness. "Cade, you have been sad ever since you got back from New York. I know you, and I can see the difference. For years I saw you surrounded by beautiful women, but somehow you showed them off like new cars. This is the first time that I have seen you breathless when describing a girl. Your eyes suddenly shine when you talk about Clover. Do you seriously want to give up this feeling? Do you know how rare it is to really fall in love?"

"Did you take any risk with Dad?"

"When we love, we are always taking some risk… but

believe me, sweetie, it's worth it."

Cade embraced his mother. "How can you be so wise?"

"Years and years of mistakes have become the experience that we pass on to future generations," she smiled. "Go ahead and jump in, love! I know you're brave enough to take some risk, and I'm sure you won't regret it."

"Clover will be immensely happy to know that you believe in her…" for a moment Cade saw her, with her red hair and big, shiny eyes, so fragile and tender, so hungry for affection.

"I don't know Clover, but I do know you: I trust your heart. So, remember, if you don't go back to confess your love to her, I will have to introduce some of your fascinating friends to her!" She laughed. "I wonder whom she may like… if I'm not mistaken, one of them lives in New York and he's really attractive… what's his name?"

"Zack," Cade mumbled. "You can't go wrong with him. Clover has met him and she was impressed." He knew that his mother was teasing him, yet just the idea of Clover with another man drove him crazy.

"Great! I should send him to her home, with a ribbon around his neck and a note… I could write, '*you are a sweet girl, you deserve someone better than my son!*'

"Ok, Mom, you've convinced me." Cade chuckled. Then he added in a serious tone, "I just hope to convince her too! She doesn't trust my words, she thinks I'm acting all the time."

"So, don't talk. Actions are far and away more important than words." She caressed his hair, just as she did when he was a child. "I'm sure you will find the way to communicate your feelings to her."

Cade kissed her. "Thank you, Mom."

"So, this means you will be in New York with us at Christmas… right?"

"Ah! Now I get it… you would drive me into anyone's arms, just to have me in New York for Christmas!" he broke into laughter. "Dad will kill me. He hoped to avoid the trip to New York…"

"I will deal with him… that grumpy hermit!"

"Do you know something? I feel like you and Clover will really get along…"

"Well then, for this very reason, don't forget to bring her to our Christmas dinner, otherwise Jake will remain the favorite son for the rest of my life!"

*

"Miss O'Brian, do you have a minute?"

Clover cursed to herself, hearing the voice of another journalist lurking outside of one of her favorite stores. It felt like persecution!

"I'm sorry. I don't have time..." she said, passing him quickly.

But the reporter didn't give up and followed her, "Just a few questions... after Cade Harrison's sudden departure, do you have any news for our readers? Have you heard from him?"

"No."

"Why? Was your relationship just a quick holiday fling? Did you have an argument?"

"I don't have anything to add," deeply annoyed, Clover, searching for a way to escape, had an idea. Staring at a point behind the journalist, she added, "Why don't you ask him! If I'm not mistaken, I just saw him crossing Times Square..."

The reporter turned around sharply to look at the square, excited about the scoop... his eyes searched through the crowd, but didn't find the actor anywhere. "Are you sure you really saw Harrison? I don't see him..." When he turned again, he realized that she had disappeared. "Damn it! She set me up!"

Clover escaped through the back door of a clothing store and headed at a quick pace towards Giftland, pulling down her hat to hide her red hair. *Your hair is too flashy to go unnoticed.* Suddenly, she remembered Cade's observation and felt a deep sense of emptiness. These sudden memories happened every day.

At first, she had felt she was going mad with pain. She had wept for days and days, crying all the tears she had held back for years, while she was trying to appear strong. She found herself sobbing in front of the Rockefeller Christmas tree or when crossing Central Park... even when she ate chocolate. A few times clients had caught her weeping. She hated to show her weakness, but in those days she had found it impossible to control herself.

After the desperation and heartbreak, she had begun to feel a

142

cold sense of apathy. It was better than despair. If she couldn't go back to the lightheartedness she felt before meeting Cade, she could at least live like nothing could touch her.

Not even the paparazzi's assaults really touched her any more. Actually, she had learned how to fool them. Easy!

What's Obama's limousine doing parked in front of Macy's?

Who on earth is that guy with Beyonce?

Shit! That guy is John Travolta dressed like Santa!

They always fell for it. This was New York. Seriously, there were celebrities around… the paparazzi couldn't risk missing them just to follow a girl who had been famous for ten minutes!

Immediately following the *Enquirer*'s article, many other tabloids were interested in the Prince of Hollywood's new victim. The reporters were prowling around outside her house or in front of Giftland. One time she even had to call the police! She had resolutely refused to answer any questions, but it didn't work.

Two days after Cade's departure, the *Enquirer* published some images of her. She was walking with her head down, dressed in black, with a very pale face… she looked in mourning. They titled the piece, *the abandoned personal shopper cries for her prince…* She got so angry that she stopped wearing black or anything dark for that matter! Of course she was suffering, but she didn't want to show her intimate feelings to the whole world. Most of all, she hoped that those pathetic images hadn't reached LA and Cade!

The following week a young journalist had fooled her. He had made an appointment with her with the excuse of shopping for Christmas gifts. The thought of how easily that freckled kid had outsmarted her still stung. He asked her a few questions in a very clever way. Thank god, she was already in her resignation phase, so her answers hadn't been too interesting for the reporter, and no tears had rolled down her face. However, even from her vague answers, the tabloid had put together an article in which she seemed completely indifferent to Cade.

> A star like him, super rich and desired, could never have anything to do with a girl like me. I was just lucky to have him as a neighbor for a few weeks. Somehow, we had been helpful to each other. Cade Harrison has quickly solved his problem for family's Christmas gifts, and his fame was great publicity for our store.

But these words didn't fool too many people, perhaps because the truth was written on her face. For example, the little Stevensons had told her that she wasn't fun any more and her eyes looked empty. Well, that was how she felt: empty and lifeless.

She focused on her work more than usual, but she didn't feel enthusiastic about it and the Christmas magic she used to love so much... gone.

When she had met Cade, she had felt unconsciously that it was the realization of a beautiful fairy tale. But when he had disappeared, all her other dreams and beliefs had come down like a house of cards.

She couldn't find anything meaningful in her life... except her good friends Zoe, Liberty and Eric. They were doing everything in their power to help her to climb out of her deep hole of despair. They were very affectionate and caring, with cuddles and lots of attention.

Eric was like a brother, warm and protective, giving her a shoulder to cry on. After all, there was no one else who could understand the feeling of unrequited love better. He represented the father she had lost and the brother she wasn't close to any more.

Zoe made her laugh. She was so funny. But Clover sensed that she was forcing herself to keep everything light, avoiding serious matters. But then again, she did appreciate the way Zoe's idle chatter helped distract her. Zoe was convinced that laughing was the best cure for a broken heart – and that she could help Clover to move on by introducing her to lots of new guys. Clover couldn't even imagine dating any man who wasn't Cade – especially now – but she went along with Zoe's schemes... It was a way to keep her mind busy.

Liberty, for her part, urged her to fight back depression and sadness. She had an almost maternal attitude, and encouraged her to focus on more important things than love. She considered romantic love too abstract, almost dangerous. It was funny, since the thirty-year-old blonde had been engaged for several years. But she had explained to Clover that the kind of love, unreal, passionate and crazy – like her love for Cade – would lead nowhere. If she wanted someone by her side, a real partner, she should look for a man who made her feel serene and protected, like Justin made her feel.

Thank god she had her friends in this very difficult time. They were the closest thing to a family she had ever had.

It was Christmas Eve, and Liberty had invited her over to spend the evening together. Her fiancée was in Toronto for business, and she didn't want to go to Chicago by herself to spend Christmas with her parents. So the plan was to go to the theatre to see *The Nutcracker*, and then spend the rest of the evening at Liberty's loft in Brooklyn. Even though she wasn't really in the spirit of celebrating, Clover was happy not to have to spend that evening alone.

So, so when she had finished her afternoon of last minute shopping with clients, she went back to the store trying to be positive, and ready to have a pleasant evening with Liberty. But when she saw her friends with serious and sorry faces, she understood that something had gone wrong.

"Why the long faces? Has someone died?" she said, trying to defuse the situation, while taking off her woolly hat.

"Not yet, but it will happen in less than two hours. I will die of boredom at the Christmas Eve dinner organized by my big family!" Zoe sighed heavily.

"Come on! Family reunions are not so bad..." she would pay for a warm family with which to celebrate with! "Anyway, you can always join Lib and me after you're done with your duty of being a good daughter and favorite grandchild..."

Liberty's guilty expression stopped her.

"About our evening together..." Liberty began, looking very embarrassed, "I have a serious problem to solve with my parents and I need to leave tonight for Chicago. My flight leaves in three hours, so I really can't come to the theatre with you... I'm so sorry. You can't imagine how mortified I am."

Clover felt some tenderness, seeing her friend in such an uncomfortable state. Liberty Allen was always very organized and under control. She never had to change her plans.

"Really? Are you, my surrogate mom, going to abandon me on Christmas Eve?" she joked, collapsing into a chair. "I won't ever forgive you!"

"Please, don't make me feel even worse than I feel already. I know I had promised, but..." Liberty bit her lip.

"I'm teasing you, Lib! Relax and don't worry, I won't die of solitude. I have survived many Christmas Eves by myself..." Clover gave her a half a smile. "I will go home, order Chinese takeout and will wait for midnight to open your gifts."

Zoe came over to Liberty, looking at her with a disapproving expression. "Can't your parents wait for just one more day? Leaving Clover alone this very evening is cruel!"

"Stop it!" Liberty whispered, shooting her a dirty look.

"Clover, honey, do you want to join me and my family? I get always so bored at these reunions, you know. They are all old people and they always torment me because I'm not married yet. I don't want to hear over and over again that at my age they already had two children each!" Zoe rolled her eyes at the very thought, then she looked at Clover with attentive and sweet eyes. "Come with me, Clo. We can get drunk, while my grandma is cooking her delicious dishes. Then we can run away, when she falls asleep in her chair..."

Clover shook her head with determination. "No, no... thank you! I'm not so desperate as to crash some intimate family dinner... but thanks again," she stood up. "Well, I think I will head home now."

Liberty gave a quick glance at her watch, before exchanging a knowing look with Eric and Zoe. "Why don't we have a toast before closing? Since we are all spending Christmas separately we should take a moment just for the four of us..."

While Zoe was looking for the glasses, Eric opened a bottle of champagne, a gift from one of their customers. They toasted and kissed several times, but the atmosphere was somehow tense and heavy. Eventually, an awkward silence fell over the room.

Clover gulped down her glass in one swallow, then she put it on the table with a little too much energy. Feeling her friends' anxious gazes, she asked, "What's going on?"

"Are you sure you're feeling well?" Zoe asked in a worried tone.

"Listen guys, please stop with your funeral faces!" she huffed. "I have had better moments in my life, it's true. But I'm not going to commit suicide or become an alcoholic," she looked at the three solemn faces in front of her, and added, "We all knew from the beginning that it wouldn't last. It wasn't a surprise for anybody. Cade went back to his life and I to mine. End of story. I had a very good time, although I'm paying now for every single moment of joy I had. But it will pass soon. You know me. My dramas never last too long."

"Listen Clover, if later you feel extremely... *sad*, please call us. We'll figure something out." Liberty said apprehensively.

"No need. I will be ok!" Clover put on her woolly hat and headed to the door. "Merry Christmas guys! See you in two days..."

"Call me tomorrow!" Zoe said, walking with her to the door.

"Actually, call us even in the middle of the night, if you need to let off steam!" Eric smiled at her.

Clover laughed softly. "And I thought I didn't have anybody who cared about me! I was wrong, I have you... and you guys are more than enough!" She teased them, leaving.

Once she got out, she could finally stop pretending to smile. She pulled up her jacket collar and began to walk slowly towards the taxi stand. She was trying not to cry until she got safely home.

Liberty, Zoe and Eric watched as their friend walked away in the snow without a word. Only when they saw her disappear, did they go back into the store.

"This had better be worth it!" Liberty took her cell and dialled a number that she had quickly written on a post-it, "Otherwise, I swear, I will kill him..."

"Did you notice her eyes? They were so sad," Zoe sighed. "For a second I almost hoped that she would accept my invitation. The idea of leaving her at a time like this is unbearable to me."

"You just wanted an ally to face your family reunion..." Eric mumbled.

"It's not true! I care about Clover so much! I don't want to see her suffer..."

"Zoe, you've risked messing up the whole plan with your invitation. What would you have done if she had accepted?"

"I knew that she wouldn't accept... she's so proud. She prefers being by herself to feeling like a third wheel in the midst of a big close family like mine. It would have reminded her of her own family who are now probably celebrating without her. If I had people like that in my life, I don't know what I would do..."

"You seem to forget that in less than one hour she might well be with *someone* and not sad at all." Eric tried to be positive, but added. "However, I'm still not sure it was a good idea to go along with *his* plan."

147

"Of course! For you no man ever deserves a second chance!"

"And for you, on the contrary, they all deserve a second, a third – even several chances!"

"She just left." Liberty's voice on the phone interrupted their argument. "She said she was going straight home, but she may change her mind, I can't predict it. And yet, on the other hand, you deserve to wait in the snow for a long time!" She listened to a brief answer and said, with a half-smile, "Good luck, then."

"What did he say?" Zoe asked curiously.

"That freezing under the snow is the thing that scares him the least at the moment." Liberty shrugged. "Well, we did our part. Now we can only wait and hope all goes well. Let's go home."

Zoe nodded and grabbing her coat, with a naughty smile asked Eric, "Do you have plans for tonight? My family reunion will be deadly boring without a friend."

*

The taxi was moving slowly in the snow, but inside it was warm and the driver friendly. On a different occasion Clover would enjoy the situation and would chat to this nice man, but this evening she wasn't in the mood to enjoy being sociable.

Despite her everyday efforts to look positive and cheerful, she couldn't find one single reason to smile sincerely. It wasn't the first time she had spent Christmas Eve by herself, but usually she was able to invent something fun to help with her loneliness. But in the last two weeks her melancholy side had taken over… blame it on Cade Harrison!

She had known from the beginning that it couldn't work between them. Yet, even if her rational side was convinced of it, her heart still had a different opinion.

Silly, romantic human muscle! She thought.

She needed to do something to change herself, to stop being so naïve. Hope, daydreams, Christmas magic… they were all wonderful things, but completely insubstantial. She had to become more realistic. Every year she hoped for something that never happened. Yet she couldn't give up her optimism. How many more shattered illusions could her heart still endure?

She thought of Cade's beautiful face, illuminated by his deep, blue eyes. After he left, her heart had broken into a million pieces. Further illusions? Not any more.

The notes of *Christmas – Baby, Please Come Home*, coming from the radio, made her sigh. The sensual voice of Michael Bublè seemed to echo all her thoughts. Christmas, the snow, the lights and the music, all lost their magic without that special loved one. Her eyes filled with tears, but she didn't want to cry in front of the taxi driver. Actually, she didn't want to cry at all…

Walking slowly along the path, towards her gate, she thought, *is it possible to fall in love in such a short time?* Given how intense her emotions had been with Cade and how painful the abandonment felt, her answer was *yes*. Her days with him had been unique. Moments that had suddenly given a deep meaning to all her past hopes and daydreams. She thought that it was exactly what she had waited for her whole life. For the first time she had felt a sense of fulfilment.

Now she knew what love was. Just to be brushed by it had filled her with joy. It would be hard to find hope, enthusiasm and optimism again, but she couldn't give up. She had another year before next Christmas. Maybe by that time she would be ready for a new wish.

"It was wonderful while it lasted," she told herself, lifting up her face to the snowflakes. She would keep these memories, as something precious and rare. After all, Christmas too is brief, lasting only a few days, but we don't love it any the less for that.

She looked at the soft lights around her windows and pushed the gate, too deep in thought to realize it was already open. She had almost arrived at her front steps, when a figure suddenly appeared in front of her. She jumped with fright and immediately thought he was a burglar. She had just read in the paper that robberies were very common during the Christmas holidays, and she was a woman living alone.

"Go away or I'll call the police!" she shouted. Then suddenly her anger made her reckless. Blindly swinging her purse at the figure, trying to deliver some heavy blows, she cursed, "Damn it! It's Christmas! Don't you have anything better to do? As if it wasn't already hard enough to go back to an empty house. You could have saved yourself some bruises, you won't find anything valuable in my house!"

"I'm sorry, but you're mistaken. There's *you*."

Two strong, warm hands held her wrists to stop her. But it wasn't necessary, since that deep and slightly amused voice had already calmed her down.

"I knew I took a risk coming back here. But I sure as hell didn't expect to be attacked!"

With her heart racing, Clover tried to distinguish his features in the dark.

"Cade?"

He moved closer to the light in the window so she could see him, "Yes."

"What are you doing here?"

"I was waiting for you."

Incredulous and emotional, Clover stared at him, then she mumbled, "I had plans to be out for dinner tonight. You were risking being out here in the cold for hours… maybe all night!" Then she saw the amusement in his eyes and suddenly understood. "Liberty!" She exclaimed. "You made a deal with her… right? I will kill her!"

"It hasn't been easy to convince her. Believe me."

"Convince her of what?"

"To leave you alone on Christmas Eve, so you would come home…"

"To find you on my door step scaring me to death!" Clover moved back. Yes, she was incredibly happy to have him in front of her. It seemed as though her immense desire had somehow made him materialize in her garden. But at the same time, she was also deeply confused. She didn't want any more illusions.

Cautiously, she asked, "Why are you here?"

"For many reasons, but I don't know how to begin…"

Clover crossed her arms, "Begin with the most important."

"I love you."

She remained completely still, open mouthed.

"I wanted to tell you this last, but if I have to follow things in a certain order of importance…"

"Do *you*… love *me*? Are you sure?" She stuttered, feeling a roar in her ears.

"I would like to say *yes*. But honestly I've never felt like this before, so I don't know what I *should* feel… I trust my instincts."

"You've never felt like this… *like this*, how do you mean?"

150

Cade bent to pick up something on the ground, and then, all of a sudden, everything lit up! Every tree, fence, and walls all around shone with thousands of tiny colored lights.

"Like this!" Cade's voice was breaking with emotion. "You light my life up, Clover O'Brian."

Clover was without words. She kept looking around, amazed, all those lights reflecting in her big eyes. She felt a lump in her throat.

"I hope this gives you some idea of how I feel... When my mother suggested that I *do* something – something concrete to show my feelings for you, Christmas lights were the first thing that came to my mind. I know that you don't trust my words."

Clover bit her lip. "I'm sorry for what I said that day. I was out of my mind... I couldn't think straight."

"I couldn't think straight either, when I tried to diffuse the gossip from that stupid article. It was just an attempt to protect you. Believe me." Cade took her chin in his hands to look into her eyes. "Everything was so new and exciting between us. I just wanted to enjoy our feelings without anyone getting in our way. You told me you hated this part of my life, and I tried to keep the paparazzi away from you. I didn't want to diminish you and what was happening between us."

"It doesn't matter any more..."

"It *does* matter. I should have reassured you immediately, but when you got so angry, you turned into a wildcat! It's hard to stop you. Your words hurt me more than you can imagine. I was confused and I didn't react quickly enough."

"I didn't believe a single word of what I said."

Cade caressed her face, looking at her with an intense, deep gaze. "Also when you said that it couldn't work between us?"

Clover hesitated and Cade came closer to her. "I believe it *will* work. I have had a full, eventful life, but I've never felt so real and complete since I met you. I want to have you by my side all the time. I know that my life is difficult and chaotic, but I will do everything possible to make things easy for you."

"Wow..." Clover swallowed, with tears of joy in her eyes.

He seemed to misinterpret her reaction, and pulled her even closer. "Please, trust me. I'm not acting."

"I believe you... it's that... it's too good to be true."

"But it's all true. Ask my mother!"

"Your mother?!"

"Yes… she lectured me like she never has before! She couldn't see me staying home like a hermit, feeling sorry for myself. She even threatened to send you Zack as a gift, if I kept being so stupid…"

Clover giggled, somehow pleased to feel jealousy in his tone. "I should take that offer as a compensation for the two weeks of hell you gave me!"

Cade held her hands behind her back pulling her towards him, and before kissing her, he said, "I won't leave you any time to think about it!"

Clover opened her lips slightly as she melted into his kiss. She still couldn't believe it. She was afraid she would wake up from one of her daydreams and find herself in the snow, hugging a tree! But that warm strong body, that familiar scent, and the taste of those lips were too real to be just a fantasy.

They both opened their eyes at the same time, as they looked at each other. "You're the most unexpected gift I could ever ask for," she whispered to his soft lips.

Cade pretended to feel relieved. "I'm glad to hear that, since I didn't have time to find a real present for you! I just arrived this morning and started to organize everything… but I have a little thing for you," he put a hand in his pocket and took out a snow globe. Clover looked at it and burst out laughing. Inside the globe there was a Santa Claus in a bathing suit surfing big blue waves surrounded by green palms. On the wood base was written, *Merry Christmas from Los Angeles.*

"You didn't forget," she whispered, holding the souvenir to her heart.

"I haven't forgotten anything, Clover," he embraced her tightly. "However, I promise, I will soon have a real gift for you."

Clover smiled, looking again at the thousands of little Christmas lights all around her. "Ok, this time I will forgive you!"

"There is another thing I need to tell you…" Cade pointed at his friend's house, where he was a guest just two weeks ago. "Philip had his alarm activated and we are under the surveillance of the security camera. It has filmed everything."

Clover widened her eyes, "Everything?! Do you mean all my embarrassing slip-ups, my horrible look in the morning when I bring the trash out…?"

Cade laughed. "No! I asked him to activate it only for tonight."

"Why?"

"Because this recording, if you agree, will end up in the hands of the journalists." Cade's voice became husky, "I want everybody to know the woman I want for my partner, to share my life. It's going to create some major chaos, I warn you. There will be paparazzi lurking here every day and we will be followed for a while. Yet, gradually, they will lose interest and their curiosity will fade away – then we'll be able to have an almost peaceful life. I promise you."

"Oh my god! I love Cade Harrison and he loves me… I think I'm going to faint."

He went over to her to kiss her again. They remained in an embrace for a long time, surrounded by colorful lights and snowflakes. They could hear the bells chiming from afar.

Clover was over the moon. After all, the magic of Christmas hadn't disappointed her. Cade was in love with her and he would announce it to the whole world. She would pinch herself later to be sure she was really awake!

Then, all of a sudden she remembered something. "Cade?"

"Yes?"

"We need to edit out a part of the surveillance video before sending it to the papers," she buried her face on his shoulder.

"Why?"

"You're not going to let the whole country know that I beat you up with my purse, right?"

Cade's laugh resonated through the quiet snow-covered street.

Epilogue

This time is official: Cade Harrison is in love!

News has just arrived here at our newspaper this morning by the way of a surveillance video sent by an anonymous resident of Staten Island. The short film shows the Prince of Hollywood and the beautiful personal shopper swearing eternal love to each other!

The actor confesses to our readers, "At the beginning I was trying to divert the attention of the media so that Clover and I could have a little more time. We wanted to understand what was happening between us. She is not a woman hunting for publicity or fame, and I wanted to protect her. My success sometimes can make things difficult, especially at the beginning of a new relationship. Therefore, I hope that readers and fans will understand our desire for privacy and intimacy."

However, judging from the video, Ms O'Brian seems to be pretty good at defending herself, even when armed with just a purse... "She didn't expect to see me there! She thought I was a burglar and she acted accordingly." Cade Harrison laughed, recalling the episode. "Anyway, I think I probably deserved those blows. If nothing else, because I waited for two long weeks before confessing that I love her."

So, the most desired and courted Hollywood bachelor seems to have become unavailable. He is the forbidden dream of enthusiastic fans and gorgeous celebrities...

how did the charming, red-headed *girl-next-door* succeed where all the others have failed?

Harrison gave us an answer: "Clover is a unique person. She is the most beautiful, sweet and honest woman I've ever met. She is an outspoken and funny creature who makes me laugh like nobody else does. I hope to make her happy for the rest of our lives."

While Cade Harrison has spoken openly and without restrain about his feelings for the mysterious red-head, Clover O'Brian's discretion and sense of privacy made our work more difficult. Yet, after following her for several days around the streets of New York, we succeeded in obtaining a comment about this romantic encounter.

"Cade's love is the most magnificent Christmas gift I could ever receive," Ms O'Brian said, as she kept on walking. "It still feels impossible that he has really chosen me. My wish is to live our love without interferences and I hope it will last forever. And... since you are here," she added, before running away, "Please, write and tell everyone that from now on I would prefer that no fan would expose her butt to be signed by him. Thank you!"

We hope you enjoyed this book!

More addictive fiction from Aria:

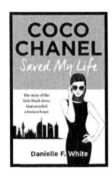  

Find out more
http://headofzeus.com/books/isbn/9781784978877

Find out more
http://headofzeus.com/books/isbn/9781784978945

Find out more
http://headofzeus.com/books/isbn/9781784975869

Acknowledgements

I've imagined this moment for half of my life, and now that I find myself here, in front of the fateful page of acknowledgements... I don't know how to begin! So, I'm not sure I will follow a hierarchy of importance. Please, don't get offended if I don't follow the right order or if I forget someone.

The biggest thank-you goes to everyone who has been close to me throughout this adventure. People who never laughed at me with disbelief when I expressed my desire of becoming a writer. On the contrary, they have always encouraged me to try. I know, there is still a long way to go, but this book is a first and very important step towards that direction.

I thank my sister, Stefania, who has always read my work with objectivity. She has never been a fan of the genre; the first romantic novel she has read is mine. The fact that she read it several times, like the Harry Potter series, has given me great satisfaction!

Thank you to Luca because, when my dream began to take off, he was with me. For years he has shared all my doubts and anxieties, but he has never given up his support and belief in me. (You did want public praise for your patience? Here it is!)

Many thanks to Battina, who helped me contain my paranoia for so many years. (They will make you a saint!)

A thanks from my heart to all my virtual friends on Facebook. You have been so sweet and supporting! (A special thanks to Maria – from my hometown – who kindly answered my many rookie questions). And a warm thanks to the girls of my favorite blogs – *La mia biblioteca romantica* and *Immergiti in un mondo... Rosa!* – who, with their positive comments about my first short stories, have given me the courage to jump in the mix.

Thank to everybody who purchased the first digital version of my book. If I am here now, it's because of you.

A huge big thanks to Newton Compton, especially to

Gabriele, Martina and Alessandra, for your trust, patience and availability, and because you taught me a lot.

And thanks also to all those who *didn't* like, accept and sustain me. Perhaps without you, I wouldn't have understood how wonderful it is to take refuge in dreams.

About Cassie Rocca

CASSIE ROCCA is a writer of Sicilian origin who has lived in Genoa since the age of three. In everyday life she is a child-minder, a job which gives her plenty of ideas for her modern fairy tales.

Find me on Twitter
https://twitter.com/CassieRocca?lang=en-gb

Find me on Facebook
https://www.facebook.com/CassandraRoccaScrittrice/

Become an Aria Addict

Aria is the new digital-first fiction imprint from Head of Zeus.

It's Aria's ambition to discover and publish tomorrow's superstars, targeting fiction addicts and readers keen to discover new and exciting authors.

Aria will publish a variety of genres under the commercial fiction umbrella such as women's fiction, crime, thrillers, historical fiction, saga and erotica.

So, whether you're a budding writer looking for a publisher or an avid reader looking for something to escape with – Aria will have something for you.

Get in touch: aria@headofzeus.com

Become an Aria Addict
http://www.ariafiction.com

Find us on Twitter
https://twitter.com/Aria_Fiction

Find us on Facebook
http://www.facebook.com/ariafiction

Find us on BookGrail
http://www.bookgrail.com/store/aria/

Addictive Fiction

First published in Italy in 2015 by Newton Compton

First published in the UK in 2016 by Aria, an imprint of Head of Zeus Ltd

9 7 5 3 1 2 4 6 8

A CIP catalogue record for this book is available from the British Library.

ISBN (E) 9781784978891

Aria
Clerkenwell House
45-47 Clerkenwell Green
London EC1R 0HT

www.ariafiction.com

Printed in Great Britain
by Amazon